SAY YOU LOVE ME

CHARLIE & ANGEL

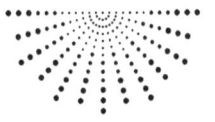

Z.L. ARKADIE

Z.L. ARKADIE BOOKS

ISBN: 978-1-942857-14-3

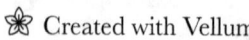 Created with Vellum

ACKNOWLEDGMENTS

Thanks to the following:

    Edited by Red Adept Editing

    Cover Design by Z.L. Arkadie Books

CHAPTER ONE

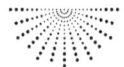

CHARLIE LORD

I park alongside the curb on Sunset Boulevard and turn off my engine.

"That sounds like a great plan." I try to force myself to smile, but it's hard. The air conditioner is on the highest setting and blowing an arctic wind into the cab of my car, but I'm still sweating bullets.

Angel sighs heavily. "She's so toxic, and I don't understand why she always gives me attitude. Granted, she was boning Papa for a while. Maybe she's mad because I never agreed with their relationship. How many times have I warned Papa about screwing the talent?"

"I don't know." I fidget nervously against the leather seats. I want to say in Jacques's defense that he rarely fucks around with the talent, but Mita

Capelli is a special case. The more I've gotten to know her, the more I've learned that it was a mistake to engage with her in the first place. She snacks on men—the wealthier, the tastier. She has long, silky black hair, creamy tan skin, and curves galore. Hardly any man could resist going for a dip in her deep, hot, wet well. I resisted up until a slight moment of weakness, when I let her spread her legs on top of me and sit on my dick. It didn't even last half a minute. Hell, I didn't even enjoy it. All I could think about was losing the only woman I could ever love, so I found my common sense, and I pushed her off me. She didn't like the rejection, and now Mita Capelli wants me to pay for my minor lapse in judgment.

"Babe, why don't you just come home?" I ask.

"What?" Angel says as if I asked her to swan dive off the London Bridge.

I rub my eyes. I can't believe I said that. Or maybe I can. Two days after Maggie and Vince's wedding, Angel flew to London to star in a musical called *The Dazzler* for a month, six shows per week. I wasn't okay with her leaving. I'm tired of us spending time apart. Then to make shit worse, four days in, Angel called to complain about Mita Capelli, the cellist. I nearly shit myself when she told me Mita was part of the live orchestra.

About three months ago, Mita sent me a letter, saying I'm the father of her child. How the hell could that have happened? I never came inside her. In the letter, she told me to pay her $20,000 a month or else. For certain, I didn't get her pregnant. So I consulted with Maggie, and she said I could call Mita's bluff and tell Angelina what happened. I was planning to call her bluff until last week.

I'm scoring a film at Jacques's Hancock Park studio. Two days ago, a package arrived, addressed to me. I opened the manila envelope, and inside was a single flash drive. I figured Jacques had sent some harmonies he thought I should use in the film. I plugged the drive into my computer. There was a single file titled "fuck." I thought it was strange, but I double clicked on it anyway, and a video of me fucking Mita opened. I was waiting for it to end after ten or twenty seconds, but the act went on for five minutes and twenty-three seconds. It even looked as if I had come.

I checked behind each shoulder to make sure I was alone. To my relief, I was. I sat there for a long time, studying the moving images on the screen, wondering how in the hell she made it look that credible. After a while, I called Maggie, who instructed me to upload the video to a secure landing page. Shortly after, she called and asked me to meet here.

Still holding the phone, I turn toward the sidewalk and gaze up at the office building. "I miss you, that's all."

"Ah," Angel says sweetly. "I miss you too, honey."

I check my watch. I'm five minutes late, and knowing Maggie, she won't be happy about it. "Listen, I have to go."

"Where are you—at the studio?"

Damn. I don't want to keep lying to her. The fact that I'm here is a result of the only lie I ever told her. "Yeah."

"Tell everyone I said hi." Angel sounds chipper, and that's a good sign. I'm guessing that Mita won't screw with our relationship—not when she thinks there's a chance she'll get her twenty thousand a month.

I tighten my jaw as I sigh quietly. "I will."

"And hey," we say at the same time.

Angel chuckles. "You first."

"I still want to talk about all the time we spend away from each other. I'm sick of it," I say.

I can hear her hesitancy in the silence.

"I was just going to say good luck," she says.

We're silent again, and that means she's avoiding giving me a response.

"Will you give it some thought?" I ask.

"Give what some thought?"

"Less traveling. More togetherness. I miss you—all the fucking time."

She sighs hard. "Charlie, it's not like I'm lolly-gagging. And you can come to London any time you want."

I bite my tongue to avoid another argument. Angel and I do that now—we argue over stupid shit like her not being able to repeat what I say verbatim, in which case I accuse her of purposely not listening to me. We argue over whether or not she or I left a cabinet door open. The quarrel we had before she left for London was her forgetting to pay the gardener on the previous day. We've considered a session with Jack and Daisy's marriage counselor, Dr. Luc Calvet. He's the guy in France, and he did a good job helping them get back on track. And he even does sessions via Skype.

My phone buzzes because I'm receiving another call from Maggie. "Okay, we'll pick this conversation up later."

"Whatever," she says sharply. "Charlie, you knew I was a dancer before you got into this with me."

"I know."

The phone beeps again.

"I love you more than dancing, though, so please don't ask me to give it up, at least for now, because…"

"Angel, I'm not asking…" The phone beeps a third time. "I'll call you later, okay?"

She's silent for a moment. "Okay," she says softly.

We say, "I love you" one last time before we hang up. Then I answer the call.

"I'm outside and on my way up," I say to Maggie.

"Then hurry." She ends the call.

I close my eyes and take a deep breath. Fucking life—sometimes it's good, but mostly, it's out to get you.

CHAPTER TWO

CHARLIE LORD

*T*he air flowing through the carpeted hallway is crisp and cool. The temperature cools the sweat on my skin, and it has a calming effect on me. I stop in front of office number 708, turn the knob, and walk inside.

I flinch, taken aback. "Whoa."

Maggie rolls her eyes as she runs a hand through her shoulder-length hair. "It's not a big deal. It's just hair dye."

She's colored her blond hair brown.

I shrug. "It's different, but you still look fine."

"Thanks for your unsolicited opinion." She points a hand at the seat across from where she's sitting. "Sit, and let's get down to business."

I look around this simple office. There's nothing

in it but Maggie's large wooden desk, her black-leather executive-style chair, and colorful, abstract hangings on the right and left walls.

I sit. "Is this where you work now?"

She pushes a sheet of paper in front of me. "Sometimes."

"What's that?"

"A report on the video Mita Capelli sent you." She smashes a finger on the top line. "This is the important part."

I pick up the page and read, "Authenticity—three percent."

"Only three percent is unmanipulated from an original source, and it's seventeen seconds long. But I take it you knew that."

I nod stiffly.

Maggie looks thoughtful. "As I remember it, Angel doesn't know about you and Little Miss Temptress?"

My chest is tight, and my head feels like I walked into a cloud of helium. "No. She doesn't."

"And you're not going to tell her?"

I round my tight shoulders to loosen them. "Remember when Angel walked in on Monroe and me? She was, you know…"

"Blowing you?"

I sigh hard. "Yeah."

Maggie groans as if the memory is causing her excruciating pain.

"So that was one big fuckup under my belt. I don't want her to know that I had two. She might think I have a problem controlling my dick or something."

"Do you?"

I flinch. "No, Mags. Jeez. Why did you ask me that?"

"Just putting it on the record."

"Well, I love Angel, and I would never cheat on her, ever."

Maggie studies me with one eye narrowed. Finally, she sighs forcefully, sits back in her seat, and crosses her arms. "Then just tell her the truth."

"What? Hell no." I'm adamant about it. "I had too many opportunities to do that, and now it's too late. She'll fucking leave me in the dust if I tell her now or if she finds out about it from somebody else."

Maggie steeples her hands under her chin and frowns contemplatively. After a number of seconds, she sighs. "Fuck, how did you mess this one up?" She holds up a hand. "Never mind. I understand."

"You do?" I'm shocked to not receive the full

force of Maggie's condemnation. She could call me *idiot* and *immature*, and I'd have no other recourse but to sit here and take it.

"Yeah. You were different then. You've changed, and you've been trying to prove that to Angel and the rest of us. If I were in her shoes, I would want you to keep that little indiscretion to yourself. But at the same time, I would never want to learn about it from someone else, either." She aims her chin at the sheet of paper in my hands. "Read the conclusive section at the bottom of the report."

It takes a moment before I rip my shocked gaze away from Maggie's face. I read aloud. "Male subject A ceased sexual activity by resisting female subject B at seventeen seconds. The deceptive value of the video begins at that time point." I grunt bitterly and set the report back on the desktop.

I squirm under the force of Maggie's narrow-eyed stare. "What you need is for Mita to stop this nonsense."

"Yeah! She's extorting me for money and using a kid that's not mine to do it."

Maggie picks up a pen and taps the butt on top of the desk. "So what you need is leverage. Something to make her keep her trap shut."

I lean forward. "Could you help me with that?"

Maggie points the pen at me. "Yes. I can."

I fall back in my chair and sigh, relieved. "How do you keep her from talking? She's in London *with* Angel right now."

Maggie wiggles her head decisively. "She's not going to say anything to Angel. You want to know why?"

I throw my hands up as if to say, *Of course.*

"Because she still wants to cash out on all the effort she's put into her investment. And you better believe someone who's gone through all of this work has some serious skeletons in her closet." Maggie smirks. "I can't wait to rattle her bones."

"Now that's the spirit." I rub my hands together. "Okay, what's our next step?"

Maggie flinches. "Our?"

"There's no way I'm going to sit around and twiddle my thumbs. I have a lot to lose here."

"Chuck. No." She shakes her head adamantly.

I slump in my seat and rub my thumb across my eyebrow. "Why not?"

"Because I got someone in mind to help."

"Who? And better yet, what the hell is going on here?" I lift my hands to indicate I mean this office.

"This is where I work when I'm in LA."

"Yeah, but what's your job officially? I thought you quit Mo&Ma PR."

"I did."

"And now?"

Maggie scratches the back of her ear. All these years, and I don't think she realizes she does it when she's under the heat lamp. "I'm on my own. I work on a case-by-case basis, and I have a client that I take on regularly."

"And you do PR?"

She sets her elbow on the desk and pinches her bottom lip. My experience tells me that means she's done talking.

I press her regardless. "Who's your one client?"

She falls back in her seat. "Do you want help with this situation or not?"

"You can't tell me exactly what you do for a living? Is what you do legal or illegal? Now I'm worried."

Once again, she scratches the back of her ear.

I propel myself forward. "Just tell me. What is it that you do?" My tone is insistent.

"Charlie…"

"Maggie."

She sighs. "Okay. But keep it to yourself."

"I will. Now, spill it."

She looks at me with skewed eyes again. She wants to tell me—I know her. Maggie and I never keep secrets from each other for long. That's the nature of our relationship. "I work for Jack mostly."

I grunt and throw my hands up. "Why so secretive about that?"

But then again, I always suspected Jack had some sort of secret life—especially when it came to business. I've entertained the idea that he's a mob guy, but crime isn't his style. But Jack has always gotten shit done too easily. I remember the state was coming after me for running a steamship service from Boston to Martha's Vineyard without the appropriate licensing. I told Jack, and within a matter of days, the threats, court dates, and astronomical fees just went away.

Then there was a time I got arrested for drunk and disorderly conduct and assault on a police officer in the Village. They intended to send me to Rikers to teach me a lesson. I used my one phone call to talk to Jack, and before the guard could put me back in lockup, we made a U-turn, and I was processed out. The arrest never appeared on my record. I've had four arrests in my life, and none of them have followed me. When I was last arrested, Jack grabbed me by the collar and said, "If you're taken in again, you're doing the time—got it?" I could tell by the look in his eyes that he meant it. The only reason I didn't test his resolve was because I met Angelina shortly thereafter. Knowing her and loving her has helped bring out the best in me.

"Charlie, just leave it alone—please," Maggie says.

I pinch my lips together and study her expression. Sometimes, when I look at Maggie, I can hardly believe who I'm seeing. She's a full-grown adult—smart, savvy, and very beautiful. We used to bicker a lot, but these days, we listen to each other and say things like, "You'll be okay" and "I understand" and "I love you." I prefer the new us to the old.

I cock my head to the side. "Is Jack FBI or something?"

She grimaces while she twists her watch. "No."

She's lying, which means he *is* part of a secret governmental organization. Well, that makes sense.

"Is your work safe?"

She narrows her eyes. "Not always, but I can handle it."

"Does Vince know?"

"Yes."

I tip my head to the side. "Really?"

She sighs heavily. "Charlie, don't make me regret telling you."

I wave a hand indifferently. "Don't. Just say safe, and call me if you need a hand. I'm a black belt, remember?"

She chuckles. "I remember…"

"And listen, Mags. I just want to be a part of catching Mita. Like I said, I don't want to sit around and do nothing."

Maggie studies me. Finally, she sighs. "I, of all people, understand that. Remember what happened to Vince before our wedding?"

"I do."

"Jack knew he couldn't leave me behind. So…" She nods once. "I'll keep you close."

I slump in relief. "Thanks. So what next?"

"I have to go to the crow's nest."

"Crow's nest?"

"Wherever Mita lives. That's where I have to go."

"I'll go with you." Then I remember tomorrow's a big day in the studio. "Well, I can go the day after tomorrow."

"Charlie, the sooner the better."

"Mags, you can't do this without me."

She narrows an eye and then sighs. I can tell by

the velocity of wind she blows through her nose that she's going to give me what I want. "Okay…"

I grin, satisfied. "Okay. The day after tomorrow."

She nods as though it hurts to make the concession.

CHAPTER THREE

CHARLIE LORD

I resist calling Angel again while inching up Pacific Coast Highway. It's after midnight in London, and she has to rest for the day's show. Last week, we were up all night, talking on FaceTime. We engaged in long-distance sex, which was pretty amazing, especially when she took her top off so that I could fantasize about doing things to her perfect tits. But she didn't get a lick of sleep, and the next day, during her performance, she fell and almost sprained her ankle. We haven't had phone sex since, and my dick feels neglected by her.

My car phone rings, and I see Angel's name on the control panel screen. I press Answer. "Hey, beautiful. Shouldn't you be asleep?" I'm grinning big.

Her chuckle sounds weary. "I didn't like the way we left things this morning. I miss you too. I miss you all the time, and I'm so dang confused about it."

That's exactly what my heart needed to hear. "Why are you confused?"

"Because I'd rather be with you than here. But..." She sighs.

"But?"

"But I'm a dancer, and I fought so hard to be what I am."

Her mother, who passed two years ago, wanted her to become a doctor. "I don't want you to stop dancing either."

The line falls silent, and for a moment, I wonder if she's still there. "Angel?"

"I'm here. Listen, babe, I love you, but I really have to get some sleep. I'll call you tomorrow."

"Of course. Oh, and is Mita still making shit tough for you?"

"Oh..." She sounds relieved. "She's gone. Thank God."

I pump my fist victoriously as I turn down my

street. This is the perfect time to hear good news. Home is less than twenty feet away.

"Good," I say.

"Great," she says.

Suddenly, the panel shows that I have another call. "Your papa is calling me."

"Oh, tell him I said hi and that I miss him," she says.

We say a final *good-bye* and *I love you*. I pull up in front of my garage as I answer his call. "Jacques!"

"How are you, son?" His voice drags as if he's tired.

"Doing well."

"Listen. I don't have a lot of time. Mita Capelli will be at the studio tomorrow. We're going to remix some of the tracks and her harmonies."

My head spins as I digest the bad news. "Mita's in LA?"

"She's on a flight from London."

I open my mouth to speak and then close it to think. My first inclination is to talk him out of using her. I discovered a better cellist—Elaine Ko from Pasadena—and if I call her, she'll definitely make herself available. But if Mita's in LA, then she's far away from Angelina, and that's the bright, shiny side of the situation.

"You do remember that Ship is scheduled to be in-studio all day tomorrow," I say. Ship Gorman is the director of the film we're scoring.

"I know, and so am I." He's videoconferencing in. "What? Do you have problem with Mita?"

"No," I say, sounding as sincere as possible.

"Shit," I mumble after we end the call. I don't want Jacques seeing me sweat because Mita's in the house. I call Maggie right away and break the news.

"Predictable," Maggie says. "She's ready to strike."

I pull into the garage, too flabbergasted to ask her to explain how she came to that conclusion. Maggie tells me that things have changed and she'll keep me posted.

"What about Italy?" I ask.

"First of all, her apartment's in Paris. And you obviously can't come now. She'll get suspicious."

"Then you're still going?"

"I certainly am."

We hang up. I sit in my car and stare at the dusty garage door. This house sits empty for most of the year. Lately, I only come to LA for work, and I normally stay in a room at the studio. But during this stint, I've been in town for six days and I've stayed here. The room at the studio has become too small for me. Life is best when Angelina and I are at home together in New Iberia or New Orleans. I've come to the conclusion that I like residing in my own home and with her in it.

I focus on the garage door. I don't want to go inside the house—at least not yet. I back out, turn my car around, and drive to Quarry, a bar off Pacific Coast Highway. I find my favorite stool and ask Mitch, my favorite bartender, to pour me a vodka and tonic.

"Been a while, brother," Mitch says as he makes my watered-down drink.

I bob my head. "So it has. How's it been going?"

"Can't complain."

Two attractive women in bikini tops and flowing skirts take the stools to my right. Mitch shrugs his forehead, sets my drink down in front of me, and leans in close, "I see you still got it."

I steal a glance at the two women. One faces the other and is grinning. I've sat through enough scenes like this to know that she's noticing me without looking and her friend is fighting the urge to turn around and get a view. I take a gulp of my drink, wondering if I should switch seats. Ever since I made a vow to be with Angel, all I want to do is run away from situations like this. Women still come on to me constantly, but I've stopped responding. I'm in love with Angel, and she's irreplaceable.

I shrug, look up at the baseball game, and slowly sip my drink. Dustin, Matt, and Corey, my Quarry bar buddies, might show up soon. I'll nurse this one drink for most of the evening while we shoot the shit. I haven't been drunk in nineteen months and plan to keep it that way.

"Boo," a woman says in my ear.

I jump and turn around. "Monroe?"

"Look who the cat dragged in."

She's wearing the same toothy smile as usual— it's just as naughty as it is nice. "Hey... I think the cat dragged you in because I was here first." I reach an arm around to hug her from the side.

Monroe rolls her eyes. "Whatever, Chuck. But really, what are you doing here? I didn't expect to see you out in LA tonight, especially without your other half."

The women on the stools to my right have decided to give us full-on eye service. Actually, it's sort of a relief to see Monroe. We both understand that we're never going to be anything more than friends, but she's mighty attractive. No woman will ever approach me if she's around me.

"I'm working at Jacques's studio," I say.

She cocks her head to the side. "Oh yeah?"

"Yeah…"

She looks so damn intrigued. I'm about to invite her to sit next to me when a couple takes the seats to my left.

"Who are you here with?" I ask.

She searches the room. "I came here to meet a potential client, who's fucking late." She turns her wrist to check her watch.

"So you're still in the smoke-and-mirrors business?"

She studies my face with a grimace. "Smoke and mirrors?" She jerks her head back. "Oh. Right. Got it. Yeah. Same business at least for now." Monroe tilts her head. "Charlie, do you have a minute? I want to talk to you about that."

I tense. "About the business you're in?"

"About the business I used to be in and now I want to be back in."

I grunt, curious. The plot always thickens when Monroe's around. "Sure, okay." I swirl on my stool and search the room for a good empty table.

"This way," Monroe says before I can spot any seats. She's already walking away.

I hop up off the stool.

"Good-bye." The woman who was facing away from me twists her body in my direction and wiggles her fingers. Her eyes are smiling and lips smirking. I smash my lips together, cut my eyes away from her face, and catch up to Monroe.

She locates a table out on the terrace with a view of the Pacific Ocean. We take our seats at the same time.

"I see women are still throwing themselves at you," she says.

I snort. "I hardly pay attention to it."

She sits back in her chair and crosses her arms and legs. "Look at you, Charlie. I thought hell would freeze over twice before you ever turned into a respectable citizen."

I laugh. "And vice versa."

"I mean, you used to be a hobo."

"And you were…" I twirl my finger next to my ear. "Cuckoo."

She laughs. "I'm still working on that."

We smile at each other. That's one thing I always liked about Monroe—she's naturally funny, which always makes for a pleasant time.

I roll my shoulders and sit up in my seat. "So what is it you want to talk about regarding your career?"

"I want to act."

I shake my head, confused. "Act as a what?"

She throws up her hands. "An actress."

"You're an actress?"

"Not yet. I want to do it, though. However, I don't want my first part to be the wrong part. You know?"

I'm still processing her big reveal. "I've never taken you for an actress. But now that I think about it..." I figure I shouldn't call her crazy again, but even the sanest actor is at least twenty- percent cracked.

Monroe is still waiting for me to finish what I was going to say.

I flop my hand aimlessly. "Forget it."

She rolls her eyes. "Forgotten." She slaps her hands and rubs them together. "So you know the right people, Chuck."

I slap my chest. "You're asking me for a job and calling me Chuck while doing it."

"Come on. You know it's a term of endearment."

I shake my head as I snicker. "Yeah... well... I'm out of the moviemaking business."

"You said you were in town working."

"Scoring a film, not casting one."

"Who's the director?"

"Ship…" Suddenly I catch her drift. "Gorman."

Monroe winks. "How well do you know him?"

Ship and I worked together three or four times in the last two years. But I've also been a guest at his house three times: one backyard barbecue and two dinner parties.

"I guess I know him pretty well," I say.

A tiny waitress with a short haircut walks up to our table and asks if we would like to order anything to eat. We decide to have dinner since Monroe's client texts that she's going to be another half hour late. Monroe speaks out loud as she types. "Don't bother. Go home. Will not represent you." She turns her phone off.

"Who was your client?" I ask.

"Peggy Dewater."

"She's an actress," I say, insinuating she should probably try asking Peggy for help, but then I think about it. As I remember it, Mo&Ma's clients are pretty fucked in the head.

"So what?" she says with a sour expression.

"Never mind." I raise a finger. "Give me a moment to think about Ship." Tomorrow's a big day. Ship will be in the studio, but we're all going to be occupied for hours. Monroe could help keep Mita in line, but first, I have to tell her what's going on.

"Why are you looking at me that way?" she asks.

Can I trust her? I stop frowning, shift in my seat, and look around to see who's in earshot. The closest table is about seven feet away. Two guys are sitting there. One keeps eyeing Monroe, but every guy out here is staring at her absentmindedly. It takes me a moment to realize how sexy she looks. I don't usually notice anymore—not because I'm so into Angel that I can't admire another attractive woman but because Monroe is like family. But she's wearing a tight grey skirt that stops just below her knees, a tight white T-shirt, and sandals, the kind with a strap around the ankle. Her long, wavy brown hair cascades freely over her shoulders and down her arms. There's not a stitch of makeup on her face, yet her skin is dewy. Monroe's originally from Manhattan, but she's transformed into a real California girl with understated sexiness.

I rub my eyebrow and move my chair closer to hers. Her forehead wrinkles as if she's concerned about what I'm going to tell her.

"Listen, Monroe. I can help you, but could I also ask you to help me?"

Her frown intensifies. "Help you with what?"

I lower my voice and give her the rundown on Mita and her blackmailing ways. By the time I make it to the end, we're huddling closer together. We only sit back to give each other space when the server brings our food to the table.

"How are you making sure she never shows Angelina that video? I don't know Angelina too well, but I gather she's a purist."

I flinch. "A purist? How?" She certainly doesn't fuck me like a purist.

Monroe starts counting down finger by finger. "She doesn't curse. She doesn't speak ill of the living. I've never heard her speak unless she has something nice to say. She's always smiling and dancing and shit, which can become kind of annoying sometimes. Sorry, but… it's true."

"Those are all things I love about her, though."

She presses down on her fifth finger. "And she's made you into a better but boring man."

I jerk my head. "Who, me? Boring?"

"Oh, come on, Charlie. You have to admit that pissing in alleys, fucking tramps, and fighting bouncers was fun."

"Not fun—stupid."

She grunts like she doesn't believe me. "You looked like you were having fun."

I study her with narrowed eyes. It's time to bring an end to the discussion of my past. That wasn't healthy behavior, nor was it fun. I was hurting deep inside, and I used every stimulant I could to keep myself from feeling the pain.

"Listen, I'm not saying you should go back to that shit. I'm just pointing out that you've found your adult because of her. Hell, that's a good thing, Chuck."

I widen my eyes. "Sure didn't sound like you thought that."

"Well, I did. So… what do you need me to do tomorrow?"

As we finish dinner, I lay out the plan. Before we leave, she points out another reason why I'm more boring than ever when I order another water and nothing alcoholic.

"Alcohol can quickly go from being your toxic friend to a harmful foe," I say.

She raises a finger pointedly. "The Premium Red Mes Fleurs can definitely be your best friend."

I laugh, but I have to agree. Jacques's vineyard churns out gnarly wine. When dinner ends, we hug and say good-bye. I'll see her again tomorrow morning. I decide to not tell Maggie about my plan to have Monroe at the studio. I'm not sure if she'd be happy about it. But for what Maggie has planned, I'm sure Monroe won't get in the way. At least, I hope she won't.

CHAPTER FOUR

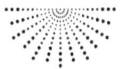

CHARLIE LORD

I make it home a few minutes after eleven o'clock. I go upstairs, flop down on the edge of the bed, and call Angel. She answers on the first ring. I tell her right away that I had dinner with Monroe and explain how we by chance ended up at Quarry.

"I'm sure she made you laugh," she says

"Yeah?" I say, surprised at her lax reaction.

"I trust you, babe. Plus, Maggie's circle of friends lives by a serious girl code. Monroe wouldn't go there even if she wanted to. She doesn't have the constitution for it."

I chuckle tiredly as I take off my pants. "I think you're right." That's another of the many reasons why I love Angel—she's observant and smart.

Angelina talks about how a scaffold was added to the stage. I lie back on the bed and struggle to keep my eyes open, listening to her give me the dimensions and height of the scaffold.

"Charlie?" she finally says.

I open my eyes, and the light of the room stabs them. Shit, I fell asleep. "Yeah?" I say in an alert voice.

"You're tired," she says understandingly. "Go to bed, sweetie. I'll talk to you tomorrow."

I want her to keep talking so that I can pretend she's sleeping beside me. I yawn. "No, I'm listening."

Her chuckle feels like a sexy whisper in my ear. I want to reach through the phone, grab her, lift her shirt off, and suck on her perfect tits.

"Go to sleep, Charlie. I'll call you... wait. You're going to be in session with Papa all day tomorrow, aren't you?"

I withhold a yawn. "Yeah." I yawn anyway.

"Then call me when you're done."

The details of tomorrow pass through my mind. My shoulders are heavier, and so is my head, thinking about how busy I'm going to be. And then there's Mita. "Will do."

We say that we love each other and end the call.

I take off my shirt and crawl into bed. All the mental stress from today comes crashing down on me. I can barely keep my eyes open as my face digs into the pillow. Before long, I can't think about Mita and the crazy game she's playing. I would give her money to make her go away. Maybe that's an option I should consider. Angel and I live on way less than I have.

Yeah, that's what I'll do. I'll pay her off.

"ABSOLUTELY NOT!"

I flinch because Maggie's voice shrieks through my speakers. I lower the volume. It's five o'clock in the morning, and I make a left on Rossmore Boulevard, getting closer to the Hancock Park studio. The tepid morning air rushes through the back windows of my jeep. It's already seventy degrees. Today's going to be a scorcher.

"If money is what she wants, I got plenty of it that I don't use or need."

"That's just ridiculous, Charlie. So you want to give it away to some lowlife extortionist?"

"No. I would rather be poor as fuck than lose Angel." The thought of losing her makes my head hurt, so I massage my temple with my nonsteering hand.

Maggie sighs sympathetically. "I know you love her. I love her too. But paying off Capelli is not the answer. I'm not going to let you do it."

"I don't know, Mags."

"Stop it, Charlie," she barks. "Everything's in place. Mita switched planes in New York. Javar was already in town and ready to make first contact."

"Make first contact? How?"

"They're on the same flight from JFK to LAX, arriving at 7:40 a.m."

I squeeze my eyes shut long enough to not lose sight of the road and miss my next turn. "How in the hell did you get her flight information?"

"Okay so… you're going to have to not ask so many questions."

What the fuck is she talking about? "What are you, Double O Seven?"

"No. I'm getting the job done. Do you want me to do that, Charlie?" she asks as if speaking to a five-year-old.

I shift uncomfortably in my seat. "Of course, but…"

"Good. Listen, I put them together just to make

sure Mita would react to Javar the way I had hoped."

One of my hands flies off the steering wheel to scratch the back of my neck. All of a sudden, I feel fidgety as hell. "And how did she react?"

"I made sure she had the worst seat in coach. When she walked through the first-class cabin, Javar was already seated and sipping champagne. I wanted her to feel the difference."

"She didn't buy herself a first-class ticket?"

Maggie snickers impishly. "She missed her original flight."

"And you had something to do with that?"

"She was held up in Customs."

"And you made that happen?"

"Yes. I did." She sounds proud of herself.

"How?" I shake my head. "Never mind."

"I wasn't going to tell you how I did it anyway."

I slap my hand back on the steering wheel. "So how did your guy do? Did she take the bait?"

"Javar sent me a text message with a thumbs-up and a ten."

"And that means?" I'm snippy, and I don't like it.

"On a scale of one to ten, Mita really liked what she saw."

I grunt sarcastically. "This guy sounds full of himself."

"Don't make this difficult, Charlie," Maggie says.

"What do you mean?"

"You're being snide, and if you want this to work, then you're going to have to lose that attitude."

I clench my jaw. "Okay. I will."

"Good. We discussed the plan yesterday, but there's one major change."

I drive down the street lined by palm trees and pull into the driveway of the 1920s Spanish-style mansion made into a recording studio. Maggie's plan still makes me nervous as hell. I've never had to put my well-being into her hands, and it's unsettling. "What's the change?" I barely say.

"You know Gill Blum, don't you?"

"Yeah. He's working on a project at the studio now."

"Since Javar made precontact with Mita, we're making it look as if he's working with Gill and not you."

I park along the edge of the long driveway, which has been expanded to accommodate ten cars while maintaining a fire lane through the middle.

"How the hell do you know Gill?"

"I know a lot of people, Charlie." Her tone is sarcastic.

I sigh heavily and rub my face. "I don't know, Mags. Are you sure this is going to work?"

"Ha! Do you think I'm just sitting on my hands over here? I'm working for *you*, Charlie. If I were any other person you hired to fix this situation, would you be asking him that question?"

I squeeze my eyes shut and then open them. Is this a fucking dream? "What the hell are you, in the first place?"

"I'm your fixer. And there are only two circumstances in which I will be requiring your input. First, if I ask for it. Second, if you see or feel something isn't going right, then call me and tell me. That's it. Understood?"

Every cell in my body wants to tell little Magnolia to kiss my ass. I'm older than she is! Not only that, but what sort of man lets his younger cousin fix his shit? I rub my eye until it itches. Common sense tells me that Maggie hasn't been little Magnolia for a long time. She's tough as nails and shrewd as hell. I heard of Mo&Ma and how just about every agent, producer, and publicist was clamoring to get a meeting with her. She's at the top of her game, and it's time I accept that.

I sigh, releasing resistance. "Understood."

"Great. Good."

Finally, I notice I'm the first one here. A chill of loneliness passes across my spine, and I shiver. "So where are you?"

"I'm in Italy with Vince."

I jerk my head. "Vince?"

"Yeah, it's this thing we're doing. Working on it, you know?"

She's not making sense. Maggie does that intentionally when she doesn't want to talk about something. She has to go before I can ask her to explain, so we say good-bye and agree to keep our phones near just in case we need to reach each other. As soon as I'm inside, I go into the kitchen and make coffee. I don't have to worry about breakfast because Lara, the studio operation manager, has arranged catering for breakfast, lunch, and dinner. Before hearing that Mita would be joining us, I was pretty excited about today's schedule. Now I'm bummed as hell.

Coffee's ready. I pour myself a cup and take it to the studio. I go right to work, preparing for today's mega-session. I power the system and play back the portion of the score we worked on yesterday. I listen to it five times and tweak some parts, getting it ready for Jacques's keen ears.

"Good morning, Charlie," Lara says from the doorway.

I quickly look at the time on the control panel. Shit, I started working two hours ago. Time always flies when I'm working.

"Morning."

"Breakfast is set up in the kitchen."

The scent of Lara's floral perfume flows into my nostrils. Angel doesn't wear perfume, but if she did, I would probably prefer a slightly toned-down version of whatever Lara has on.

"Thanks," I say.

She pulls her long black hair over her shoulder. "Big day today, huh?"

I rise to my feet. She looks up at me with dazzled eyes. I'm still nervous about coming face to face with my extorter, but I'm hungry as hell. "Yep. And now I'm ready to eat."

She chuckles. "Then go get it. I'm going to unlock the other studios."

"See you later, then," I say.

She winks and moves on.

.   .   .

I hurry to the gourmet kitchen. The scents of bacon, pancakes, and eggs compete for my attention. Two people in identical red T-shirts with white aprons are putting the finishing touches on the burners under the chafing dishes. The guy rushes out as soon as he sees me, and the girl stops what she's doing.

"Hungry?" she asks. She's probably in her early twenties.

I glance again at the stack of pancakes and rub my belly. "Yeah, I'm starving."

"Well…"

I look at her. Her skin turns red, and her smile broadens as she gives me an unsought briefing on each available food item, including what's gluten free, organic, and the different types of syrups made from fresh berries. I thank her when she's done and grab a plate.

"This looks like a really cool place to work," she says.

I press my lips into a hard line as I use the tongs to put three blueberry pancakes on my plate.

"I'm an actress." She chuckles nervously. "Like every other person in LA, right?"

I serve myself a healthy portion of scrambled

eggs and nod. "Yeah." Fucking LA. Just about everyone you meet has an angle.

"Doesn't Jacques Blanchard own this studio?"

I serve myself two slices of bacon. "Yep."

"Well then, you should give me a tour."

Her tone has changed, so I look over at her. She has taken off her apron, and all I see are the nipples of her fake tits poking through her very thin T-shirt. My eyes veer up to her suggestive smile. I always find myself in these sorts of situations. I must be sending out some kind of vibe that says, *Hit on me because I want to fuck you*.

"He's not a tour guide, babycakes." Monroe walks in and takes a plate off the top of the stack.

I shake my head, surprised to see her although I'm glad she's here. "You're early."

"Indeed I am." She narrows an eye at the girl. "And just in time, I see. Someone was this close to offering you a blow job."

The girl turns redder than before, balls up her apron, and scurries toward the exit. She walks right into Lara and a woman in a white chef's coat who looks as if she runs the entire catering operation. The guy who was in the kitchen with the girl when I first walked in is behind them.

"Oh, you found him," Lara says to Monroe.

Monroe pats my shoulder briskly. "Yep, here he is."

"You didn't tell me you had a new assistant," Lara says, addressing me.

I clear my throat. "Just for today."

Lara eyes Monroe questioningly. "All right, then." She returns to her conversation with the caterer about lunch and dinner. The girl who hit on me puts her apron back on. The head caterer tells her to bring in more selections of juices.

She darts out of the kitchen, avoiding eye contact.

Monroe snickers. "Too bad you're not still in your pussy-collecting phase. She would've definitely scored today," she whispers.

I snort and roll my eyes. "I couldn't say. She's not my type."

"That's right. You were into exotic butterflies." She flutters her arms like they're wings.

I laugh, and after fixing our plates, we walk out the tall French doors and sit at one of the round tables under the glass-enclosed patio.

"So why are you pretending to be my assistant?"

Monroe pauses before putting a forkful of scrambled eggs into her mouth. "Maggie called me last night. I'm the hot threat."

I feel completely confused.

"You don't know what that is?" she asks.

"Are you going to make me guess?"

"I should, but I'm not. I'm Mita's competition." She eats the eggs.

I tilt my head as I try to make sense out of what she just said. Suddenly, I get it. "Oh, you're the fox in the chicken coop."

Monroe swallows. "That's one way to look at it. If this Mita woman feels she has competition, she's going to try harder to land her guy."

I nod thoughtfully. I have to admit, I wanted Monroe here to keep Mita off my ass, not to push her on Javar Les's dick. I want to call Maggie and chastise her for not updating me about Monroe, but what's the use? If I want this to go away, then it's time for me to fully accept that Maggie's running the show.

"Right. So have you ever met Javar Les?" I ask.

Monroe's gaze dances around my face as she holds onto a smirk. "Are you jealous, Charlie?"

"What?" I'm shocked that she would assume that. "I may be doubtful of this guy's persuasive powers. But jealous? No way."

Monroe studies me for a moment. "Um-hum. Well, let's just say when he arrives, you will be the richest guy in the house but not the hottest. Granted, you're smoking hot, but Javar is a volcano!"

I can tell Monroe is enjoying this, so I decide to no longer engage. I nod coolly. "Whatever it takes, then."

"He certainly has what it takes."

I stop myself from rolling my eyes. "Are you and Maggie business partners again?"

Monroe's merry mood changes. "No. And I still need you to get me in front of Ship Gorman."

"You know he's married, right?"

She shrugs. "So what? I'm not going to fuck him. I just want to convince him."

"Convince him of what?"

"That he and I should work together."

"And how are you planning on doing that?"

Monroe winks.

"So that does mean you are going to fuck him?"

She groans and waves her head. "Does everyone suspect that a girl who wants to be a superstar is ready to offer up her pussy or a blow job to get there?"

"Well, you just saw what happened in the kitchen."

"I'm not her. I'm fucking Monroe Blanco, bestselling author and Emmy Award winner. I'm a fucking winner." She points her fork at me. "Remember that."

I can't help but laugh. She prattles on about the acting school she's been attending in West Hollywood. It's the number-one school in the world. At this point, I'm scarfing down my pancakes because I'm aware that Mita and Javar Les's flight has already landed and they should be here soon. But who will get here first?

Monroe goes back for more fruit and eggs. I've piled my plate high enough for at least three servings, although my appetite is not as big as it was. I place my fork on my plate and take my napkin off my lap. It's time for me to get back into the studio. "Well…"

"Hello, love," a voice says from behind. It's a guy with a British accent.

Monroe's eyes light up because she sees him first. I whip my face around. *Goodness fucking gracious…*

CHAPTER FIVE

CHARLIE LORD

*J*avar Les strolls over and flops down in a chair that's very close to Monroe. At least we're about the same height, around six foot three. His eyes are pale blue. I bet he's wearing contacts. And his long, messy hair... who does he think he is, me? Shit, I gotta find a new hairdo.

"Sorry about your woes, mate," he says.

I blink at his face, trying to push my thoughts away so I can respond to whatever the hell he just said. Has Angel ever met him? Suddenly, I'm glad Mita's here and not in London. I don't want this guy anywhere near my fiancée.

"What's that again?" I ask.

"Your woes, mate?"

"Oh. Yeah." Maggie must've filled him in.

"Listen, she's on the way. Her driver's going to text me when he's cleared traffic. I thought we should meet first, and, uh, you and I are not mates, understand?"

"Then what are we?"

"We're the opposite of mates."

I squirm in my seat and clear my thoughts. I fucking notice that when he smiles, his whole face follows suit. Should a guy notice that about another guy?

"Then we're enemies. At least, that's what you want her to think," I say.

I glance uncomfortably at Monroe, and she's grinning so hard that her face might break.

"Something like that." Javar suddenly looks down and takes his cell phone out of the pocket of his Bermuda shorts. He sets his eyes on Monroe. "It's a pleasure seeing you again." He stands and looks down at me. "We're on in twenty minutes. Could you show me to my quarters, please?"

I glance at Monroe again. She looks me in the eye, but it's like she's dazed. Also, her skin is blotchy. I think he's gotten her flustered. I've never seen her not confident.

"Right." I slowly rise to my feet. Monroe shakes herself out of her stupor. "I'll be back," I say to her.

Javar touches Monroe on the shoulder "I'll see you later?"

Monroe rips her eyes away from his curious gaze and smashes her lips together. Finally, she shrugs. "We'll see."

I study her and then him. They've definitely fucked before. I wonder if Maggie knows it. I partly want to call and ask. Whatever the hell is going on between them could probably jeopardize her whole operation, because if by some small chance they haven't fucked, they definitely want to.

I open the door to the bedroom. "It's this one."

"She normally stays here?" Javar asks.

I stiffen my neck. Suddenly, this guy has a clean American accent. "I thought you were English."

He smirks. "I'll reclaim my accent when this is over."

"All right, then. Do you need anything else from me?"

He takes off his backpack. "Not at the moment."

"Good luck." I turn to leave.

"Hey, mate," he says.

I whirl around. "Yes."

"Monroe. She's something, isn't she?" He shrugs his forehead.

I feel my forehead collapse. "What do you mean?"

He waves a hand. "Never mind. I have to prepare the room." He points at Mita's room. "And it's here, right?"

"Yes."

He points his thumb at the room across from Mita's. "I'm here?"

I nod briskly.

"Right… right."

"Okay." I turn to leave again.

"Mate."

I sigh and face him. "Yes?"

"Would you tell Monroe…?" He frowns, looking off. "Forget it."

I wait a second, just in case Javar changes his mind. He focuses on unzipping his black-leather backpack and rummaging through it. I guess that was it. This time when I leave, he doesn't stop me.

I make it back to the kitchen. Taylor, Scott, and Levi—guys on my production team—are eating breakfast at the table with Monroe. They're laughing and chatting as if they've known each other for years. I wouldn't be surprised if they have. I'm itching to join them, but we have to be in-studio in ten minutes. I grab a quick cup of coffee and stand at the counter to scarf down a small plate of turkey bacon and eggs Benedict.

"Ciao, Charlie," a familiar voice says as if we're old friends and she's not blackmailing me.

I turn to glare at Mita Capelli, standing in front of the doorway behind me. She's holding a rolling suitcase and looks surprisingly fresh for having flown from London to LA at the last minute. My mouth tightens. Should I ignore the fucking pink-polka-dot, tap-dancing elephant in the middle of the room? She still holds all the fucking cards. One call to Angelina, and my life is over. I scratch an eyebrow.

"Do you not speak?" she asks.

"There's nothing to say."

"Oh…" She grins devilishly. "We have lots to say."

Anger propels me closer to her. I stop and glance to my left, acutely aware that others may be watching us. "Stay away from me," I say, lowering my voice.

She folds her arms defiantly. "Only if you cooperate."

"What have I ever done to you?" The second I say it, I want to take it back and try over again. That sounded too vulnerable.

"You fucked me, Charlie. Now we have a child together."

"You know that's not true."

"You have seen the video, no?"

I tighten my lips. Mita turns her face up, looking at me like a mean kid on the playground. I've met tons of crazy chicks in my life, but she may be the most cracked.

Monroe's laugh rises from the patio. Mita snaps her eyes in that direction. Her mouth falls open and then closes as Monroe flips her hair across her shoulder and stands. If Monroe's putting on a show, it's a good one. I hadn't noticed her tight skirt that dips below the knees and her tight white T-shirt. She wore something like it last night at dinner. Mita's face has envy written all over it. Monroe sets her curious gaze on us and smiles. She's on her way. Mita glances at the doorway as if she wants to make a quick getaway. It's too late to run now.

Monroe steps beside me. "Ready, Boss?"

My heart is thumping like horse hooves on a racetrack. I spastically check my watch. "Yeah. Sure."

Monroe extends a hand toward Mita. "Oh, hi. I'm Monroe."

It takes a few beats, but Mita finally shakes her hand. "I am Mita Capelli. You are with us today?"

Monroe's smile is good and pleasant. "If you're working with Charlie, then yes. I'm assisting him."

"I see." Mita smiles stiffly and then strolls out of the kitchen, ensuring we get an eyeful of her ass shaking.

When she's out of view, Monroe grunts curiously.

"What is it?" I ask.

"She's definitely predictable," she mutters.

I fold my arms. "Is that a good thing?"

"What do you think?"

"I think yes."

Monroe affirms my answer with a wink.

On that note, we head to the studio. Ship Gorman is late, but we don't panic because he's never punctual. I show Monroe how to log changes, which will keep her out of the way and focused on one task for the entire session.

"Really, Charlie, that's all you have for me?"

"What else can you do?" I ask, wondering if she has any scoring skills that I'm not aware of, which wouldn't surprise me. Just when I think I know everything about Monroe, I learn something new.

"Nothing, just trying to loosen you up." She tilts her head and looks at me poignantly. "Don't worry, Charlie. Maggie isn't going to let Crazy Bitch hurt you or Angelina."

I'm about to respond with doubt, but Taylor, Scott, and Levi walk in. The musicians gather in the pit, including Mita, who has changed into a skimpy tank top and skin-tight jeans.

"I've never been so inspiring," Monroe whispers in my ear.

No explanation needed. Mita wants to be the only woman in the vicinity that makes a man's pants tight in the crotch.

Everyone is in place, and we're ready to begin. Jacques should already be on the line, but Lara hasn't hit the ready button yet. I buzz her to see what's the holdup.

"I can't reach him," Lara says. She sounds stressed.

The crew and I look at each other. Jacques has

never been late for a session, let alone missed one without rescheduling.

"Did you call his cell?" I ask.

"It's off."

"He's in Paris. Do you have the number to his flat?"

"Called there too, and the studio." I picture Lara sitting at her desk, pulling her hair out.

"Have you tried Madeleine?" I ask.

"Who?"

Madeleine is Jacques's girlfriend. They've been together for a little over three months—the news of his brand-new love interest probably hasn't made it to LA yet.

I scan all the inquisitive faces in the room. Mita and Fidel, the banjoist, are in isolation booths, fine-tuning their instruments. Ship hasn't made it yet, but he called and said he's only a few minutes away. He just cleared stop-and-go traffic on Highland Avenue.

"Lara, give me a second," I say.

She sighs. "Okay."

I switch off the conference call and take out my cell phone. Thank God Angelina made me put Madeleine's number in my contacts. She said Jacques and Madeleine have been like two peas in a pod, and because of it, Jacques has gotten into the habit of turning his phone off when he's with her. He's changed a lot since they've gotten together. He doesn't play all hours of the night and all over the world like he used to. He actually takes weekends off. He's even letting me score the entire film, *Titan Seas*, so that he can spend the entire month of August in the Galapagos Islands with Madeleine. It's going to be his first vacation in eight years.

The call makes its fifth buzz, and now I'm just waiting to leave a message. I'm also saddled with the fact that I'm going to have to lead today's session without him. There's a sixth buzz, and then a quiet voice says, "Charlie?"

I'm hit by a sense of relief. "Madeleine, ciao." I ask in French if she knows where Jacques is.

It takes her a second. Then she whimpers. *Oh, shit. Have they already broken it off?*

"He's…"

"Madeleine?"

I turn to Terry, who's watching me with a curious frown.

"What?" he mouths.

"He is in hospital," Madeleine barely says.

I shoot to my feet. "What?"

CHAPTER SIX

I excuse myself and take the call to Jacques's office. Madeleine tells me that he's been sick, but he wouldn't go to the hospital. Two days in a row, he hadn't slept or eaten because he was finishing up a project. This morning, she found him unconscious and alone in his studio. She called an ambulance and performed CPR until they arrived. So far, all the doctor could tell her about Jacques's condition was that he went into cardiac arrest but now he's stable. He couldn't give her more information because she's not family.

"I cannot contact Angelina," she says. "May you help with this?"

I close my eyes and take some deep breaths to steady myself. This seems so fucking unreal. And

Angelina… hearing that her father's in the hospital will hurt her bad. I need to be there for her.

"Yes," I say. First, I call Dongo, Jacques's older brother, since he lives in Paris. He should be able to have the doctors give Madeleine the updates she needs.

Dongo asks a bunch of questions. I can only tell him what I know, but that doesn't satisfy him. He's a gruff dude, lacking the charm and congeniality of his younger brother.

"Was he with *her*?"

I run my hand through my hair. Damn, he has me on edge. "Who's *her*?"

"The bitch."

"The bitch?"

"Madeleine," he barks.

I plant my face in my hand. "She's the one who found him and administered CPR. She saved his life."

He's silent, but I can feel his fumes snaking through the phone.

"Who told you that?"

"Um… she did." I wipe my face with my hand, realizing what he's insinuating.

"She's a liar. I want her away from my brother. Which hospital?"

Shit. I look around the room for help, but I'm the only one here. I need Angel. She knows how to control her hotheaded uncle, but she has three shows today and won't be available for hours. The only person who could possibly help me reach her is Mita. "Fuck!" I shout in my head.

"I said, which hospital?" Dongo demands.

I'm forced to give up the information. I can see it now. He's going to crawl up Madeleine's ass and grow if I don't get hold of Angel right now.

I MAKE IT BACK TO THE STUDIO. SHIP GORMAN HAS finally arrived. Monroe is already bending his ear about something. All conversation stops after I walk into the room and face everyone.

"Charlie, what's going on?" Monroe asks.

I press my fist against my lips, and she stands. *Fuck, dude, don't cry in front of all these fucking people.* I clear my throat.

"Jacques is in the hospital."

Her eyes expand.

"What for?" Levi asks.

"He went into cardiac arrest."

The room erupts in a collision of "fuck," "shit," and "what?"

It's only now that I notice Mita and Fidel are out of the booths and in the main live room, looking at me expectantly. The studio PA system is on. I try to think of anyone else who may know how to reach the director, but a bunch of names and faces clump together in my brain. Mita just left the show. She's the fastest road to getting what I need.

Ship Gorman falls back in his seat and throws his hands up. "What the hell are we supposed to do now?"

My mouth opens to speak, but hell if I know what to say.

"Charlie, what can I do for you?" Monroe says.

I scratch my head, thinking. *Get it the fuck together, Chuck.* I have to bite the hot bullet and ask for a favor from the devil herself. "I need a phone number."

"What number?"

"Angelina's director. She's in shows all day. I can't reach her until after the last show ends, but the director will be able to get a message to her now."

"Okay," Monroe says carefully.

"Mita just left the show. She should have the director's name and number."

Everyone looks at Mita, including me.

"Um…" She stands slowly. "I don't…" She grimaces as if she has to think about what she's trying to say.

Monroe slaps her hand on my shoulder as she glares at Mita, as if she's encouraging me to do what's difficult and get that number.

I lean into the microphone. "Mita, can I talk to you in Jacques's office?"

It takes her a moment. She looks at Ship and then John, my audio guy, who's out there in the live room with her.

Mita shakes her head. "I can't help you."

I hear two hard steps, and then Monroe is right beside me with her mouth close to the microphone.

"The hell you can't," she says.

I can feel the shock in the air.

Monroe thumbs over her shoulder. "Get your ass in the office, and tell Charlie how he can contact his girlfriend's director."

Mita frowns at Monroe. I don't have to guess what she's thinking—she's wondering who the hell Monroe is and why she thinks she can talk to her that way. Monroe doesn't unfold her arms or drop that murderous look in her eyes.

After a moment, Mita sighs and shakes her head. "I'll see what I can do."

Now Ship steps forward. "If you can help, then you probably should," he says, shaking his head.

"Okay. I'll go with you to the office," she says.

Monroe squeezes my shoulder. "Let me handle this." She's on her way out before I'm able to respond.

The room is still motionless. I take a deep breath and let the tension out of my body.

"Who the hell is she again?" Taylor asks.

I'm about to respond when Ships says, "That's Monroe Blanco."

Taylor snickers. "Is she your bruiser-slash-assistant or something?"

The guys chuckle as much as their worry allows.

"She can be," I say.

"Why is Monroe Blanco here in the first place?" Ship asks.

I figure there's no time better than the present to expose Monroe's true intentions for being here.

"She came to see you," I say.

"I sort of got that feeling."

"She wants to be an actress, and since you're a director…"

He frowns, baffled at first as he nods, and then his expression turns intrigued. "We'll talk."

Taylor sits farther back in his seat. "I wouldn't mind talking to her either." He shrugs his eyebrows. "If you know what I mean. But first, we gotta know how Jacques is doing. This is all so fucking surreal."

"So are we going to cancel the session today?" Ship asks.

The answer is easy. "Jacques would kick me in the balls if he knew I cancelled our session, regardless of whether he's in the hospital or not."

"That's true," Taylor says, nodding.

"So what do you think, Ship?" Levi asks.

Ship narrows his eyes shrewdly. "I think this team is capable. Let's do it."

I sigh in relief just as Monroe walks into the control room. She hands me a folded sheet of paper. "I called the director already. He's going to have Angelina call you in…"

My cell rings. I jump, and so does everyone else. I snatch my phone off the console. "Hello?"

"Charlie? What's going on? Jeremy said there was an accident or something. Are you okay?"

"Hey, babe, one second," I say, cradling the

phone to my ear as I rush out of the room to take the call in private. On the way out, I wink at Monroe to thank her.

Finally, I'm in the hallway and run into Javar Les. He walks past me as though we never met.

I walk across the marble floor behind Roman columns that separate the pathway from the living room, which has been turned into a lounge area. To move farther away from any possible disturbance, I run up the stairs, taking them three and four at a time.

"Babe, Jacques is in the hospital," I say once I reach the top.

"What? What do you mean?"

I make it to the private luxury suite. Jacques, Lara, and I are the only ones with keys. It's one of three rooms of its kind, which are reserved for bigwigs who come from out of the country or another state. I repeat what I've been told about Jacques.

"Oh God," she says as though her whole world has just come crashing down on her.

"I called Dongo because…"

Angelina groans. "No… Dongo never likes any of my father's girlfriends. He's going to give her a hard time."

"I gathered that."

"Okay…" she whispers in a familiar tone. She's calming herself so that she can go into solution mode. "I'll call Madeleine and get to Paris as soon as I can. Could you call Daisy?"

Damn it. I forgot. Daisy and Jack would want to know about this. "Sure, I'll call them now. And I'll catch the first flight I can to Paris."

"No," she cries. "Papa would want you to finish the project."

I crack a tiny smile. Now I know for sure I made the right decision to stay and finish the recording. "We'll be done by tonight. I'll fly out tomorrow." For a second, I wonder if I should clear my plan with Maggie first, but there's no way I'm going to let Angel go through this without me.

"Good," she says, sounding relieved.

Angel accepts my terms. Tomorrow, I'll see her beautiful face again and squeeze her soft, warm body. I call Daisy and update her on everything I know. She thanks me and says she'll see me in Paris. Finally, I call Maggie.

She exhales forcefully. "So Javar is going to have to work fast. I'll let him know."

"All right, then." I'm even more nervous now

than I was before the day started. "Is everything going to be okay?"

"Charlie, the best thing you can do is not worry. Call you later. I have to go."

She speaks quickly and hangs up before I can ask how she is.

I'm alone in the room, and the silence feels good. I try to think about how life would be without Angel. I can't live without her. I can't picture myself making love to another woman, not even one as hot as Monroe or that bitch Mita. Angel is it for me. I have to do whatever it takes to keep her in my life. I'll give Maggie time to work her magic, but if it comes to me having to pay Mita what she asks, then I'll just have to do it.

"Here it goes," I whisper and rub my hands together.

It's time to get focused and score this film. I head back downstairs to the studio. My phone rings before I reach the door. I look at the name.

"Hey, babe," I say.

"Quick report: I spoke with Dongo and Madeleine. Dad is fine. He also had a fever, which they brought down. Madeline said he'd been coughing and wheezing for the last five days and kept promising to go see a doctor when he was done with whatever he was working on. So basically, the doctor said he should live. He doesn't have a bad heart, and being a workaholic almost killed him." She takes a deep breath. "Also, I made Dongo promise to be nicer to Madeleine. And finally, when Dad's released, Madeleine and I have agreed that he should stay at Mes Fleurs. Maybe we can stay with him for a while. Oh, wait—it's Daisy on the other line. Talk later?"

"Absolutely. Thanks for the update. I love you."

"Love you more," she says.

"Hey, and call me if there's a change in Jacques's status."

"I will."

"Thanks, and by the way…" I smile big. "I'm the one who loves you more."

She chuckles as her line clicks again, indicating that Daisy is still trying to get through. We say good-bye for real this time, and I finish making my trip to the studio.

"So how is he?" Ship asks as soon as I walk into the control room.

I tell them everything Angel told me except for the part about Dongo and Madeleine.

"Humph," Levi says, and a stoic expression

takes over his face. "We've lost a lot of great ones that way. They worked themselves to death."

We all take a moment to ponder Levi's statement. We've all worked ourselves to sheer exhaustion at some point in time. I remember when all I did was blow my inheritance on a daily basis. Life sure has changed. I love what I do, and so does Jacques. Will I die for it?

I clap my hands and rub them together. "Should we get to it?"

They all seem to rip themselves from their thoughts.

"The sooner we start, the sooner we'll finish," Ship says.

"Ditto," I say and call people to their places.

The good work starts. When it's over, I'll be on my way to see the one person I miss the most.

CHAPTER SEVEN

MAGGIE ADAMS

I pat Vince twice on the side of his thigh. "Let's go."

We've been standing in front of a window of flat 503-C, an apartment building across the street from where Mita lives. The flat belongs to Dimitri Moreau. He's a fifty-two-year-old, twice-divorced venture capitalist with a daughter who's twenty-three and a son who's eighteen. We've been in front of Dimitri's tall window for three hours and twenty-seven minutes. At times, I sit on the brown leather sofa while Vince keeps watch, and then we switch. Mostly, he stands behind me, stroking my hips, rubbing my pussy through my jeans, and pulling my hair to one side so that he can expose my neck and gently kiss my flesh. Sometimes, I ask him to contain himself. This is not the place or time for him to make me all hot and bothered.

Vince lets go of me. "So I finally get to see you in action?"

"That is why you're here." I snatch my leather duffle bag off the floor.

"You seem bothered by it."

I stop scanning the room to make sure we don't leave any traces of ourselves behind. "I'm not. You said you wanted to see if what I do is dangerous. Well, what has been dangerous so far?" I sling my duffle bag across my shoulder.

"Breaking and entering, for one."

"I don't call it that." I take the small white box out of my pocket. "I have a key."

My husband parts his lips to speak but narrows one eye instead. I guess the argument against what I said is too complicated.

I wink. "Let's go."

He grunts a chuckle. "You're the boss."

I taught Vince the drill. We walk out like the newly married couple we are—smiley and falling all over each other. The hallway is clear. The red carpet keeps the sound of our footsteps to a minimum. We pass on taking the small elevator and opt for the staircase. It's best to make as little human contact as we can. Before I chose Dimitri Moreau's apartment as a stakeout, I used the HOME database located in the control room of Jack's jet to find out as much information as I could about who lives in all the apartments with a direct view of the entryway to Mita's front door. Dimitri, a workaholic who moved to Paris after spending the last twenty years in New York as a hedge-fund manager, was the perfect mark. Now he's a venture capitalist, and his main office is in London. That's where he spends most of the day. Currently, he's on a train, heading home. He should arrive at the station in an hour and thirty-seven minutes. By then, Vince and I will be doing something about the sexual urges he's stimulated in me while we've been on watch.

"Wait a second," Vince says.

I stop and turn just before opening the exit door. Vince tugs me into his embrace, and our mouths merge.

"You're sexy when you're in charge," Vince says breathlessly as our lips disconnect.

"And so are you." I kiss his lips quickly, rope my arm around his, and guide him out the exit. We walk through a small lobby under a twelve-foot-high domed ceiling and out into a narrow hallway—

which leads us past a flower shop on one side and a pharmacy on the other—and onto the sidewalk.

We stop before stepping onto the street so that I can check the tracker on my phone. Grey Lansing is keeping tabs on the babysitter of Mita's child through her cell signal. She's still walking in the opposite direction of the apartment.

"Still clear?" Vince asks.

"Yeah." Six times since working with Jack, I've had to go into the mark's office, home, or car to search for any information we could use against him or her, and each time is just as nerve-wracking as the first.

"Are you okay?"

I fake a confident smile. "Better than ever."

He straightens his eyebrows before joining me as I skip across the narrow cobblestone street.

This neighborhood is not inexpensive. The buildings were built hundreds of years ago and were last renovated in the late forties or early fifties after War World II, effectively maintaining the old-world charm.

Once we make it to the red-painted door, I take my universal key box out of my pocket and insert the skinny metal post into the lock. The device goes to work, forming into the shape of the lock. Within seconds, I feel the click and turn the key and knob. The door opens, and we're in.

This building has cameras in the elevators, stairwell, and hallway, but Grey has tampered with them to make the recordings appear to have stalled as soon as I turn the key. Vince and I take the elevator up to the twelfth floor. We're the only ones taking the ride. Once the elevator stops, we get out and stroll down the hallway to Mita's apartment as if we belong here. Unlike the door to the building, the apartment door takes a keycard. I open the universal key box, take the key card out, and slide it into the slot. The lock clicks on the bolt in the apartment behind us. There's no way I'm going to get the door open before Mita's neighbor comes out.

"Get all handsy, and nibble my neck," I say to Vince.

He's on it. I giggle just as the door to the apartment opens. I make brief eye contact with a thin, dark-haired woman in tight jeans, sheer white button-down blouse, and red booties.

"Bonjour," I say.

She presses her lips together in a feeble attempt to smile and looks away to avoid getting an eyeful of Vince.

"Let's not defile Mita's apartment," I say loudly and clearly.

Vince chuckles and finally gives the neighbor the attention she's been seeking. "Bonjour."

The young woman's powdered face turns red as she smiles. "Bonjour." And for his enjoyment, she walks seductively down the hallway, more than likely hoping he's still watching.

Vince puts his mouth close to my ear. "How did I do?"

"Small part but Oscar-worthy performance." I open the door and press my fingers across my lips, signaling him to stay quiet.

He does a quick salute, and we go inside. The apartment is spacious and decorated in a modern French-parlor style with two blond-leather chaise lounges on either side of the fire-place, a spotless, smudgeless glass coffee table in the middle, a baby grand piano in one corner of the room, and window benches along a bright atrium that looks over the main avenue. Basically, this place is spectacular, and there's no sign that a two-and-a-half-year-old lives here or just left. I walk into the living room and set my bag on the hardwood floor next to the coffee table then unzip my bag and take out a pair of plastic gloves and a hover camera with a light on the front.

Vince throws his hands in the air and mouths, "What about me?"

I examine him. I didn't count on him participating, but since he's here, why not use him?

"One second," I mouth, and I dig another pair of gloves out of my bag and give them to him.

It's funny watching him stretch the plastic over his extra-large hands. The gloves don't even cover his palms.

Vince walks over and gathers me in his arms. He puts his mouth close to my ear. "So why do we have to whisper?" he whispers.

I put my mouth next to his ear. "Actually, no talking."

"Why?"

My lips brush his on their way to his ear. "Because we never know who's listening," I say breathlessly. Gosh, barely a kiss, and he still has the ability to make my head spin.

Vince blinks and then points toward the hallway as if to say, *After you, then.*

I steady my breath and control the dizziness as I walk to the bedroom. I've already studied the floor plan, so I know where to find it. Women usually keep their secrets in drawers or stored away in fancy boxes in their closets or under the bed. I open the drawer of the nightstand next to the bed. Panties and bras have been tossed in with condoms. I go to the nightstand on the other side of the bed and find bills, a shopping list, pay stubs, mints, hairbands, and other loose nonessential items. I study the pay stubs. Three of them are from Midnight Orleans Productions, Jacques's company, and six are from the Le Grande Symphony. The payments from Le Grande Symphony are astronomical—one for thirty grand, two for fifty grand, and three for sixty grand. I didn't know cellists were paid so well.

I open the drawer wider to see if I missed anything. Voilà. A sheet of paper folded into a square is stuck against the back of the drawer. I take it out and unfold it. It's the edge of a check stub for payment from Sir Walter Barnaby in the amount of $20,000 with "extra essentials" written in the lower left corner. I feel the back of the drawer and find more stubs, so I take pictures of all of them and send the images to Grey. Next, I take out my cell phone and text a request for him to run a search on this Sir Walter Barnaby as well as Le Grande Symphony. He sends me back a green light, which tells me that he's on it.

I turn to Vince as soon as I remember he's in the room. He shows me thumbs-up. I wink and tilt my head toward the walk-in closet. His help will surely be appreciated there. He follows me into the closet. Mita has plenty of outfits hanging on bars and shoes displayed on floating shelves. The five shelves to the right hold big, decorative cardboard boxes, each with a shiny pink ribbon on top. I go through the first box and find nothing substantial. Then I sift through the second and third boxes. I reach up to retrieve the one that's second from the top, but Vince, who's standing behind me, gets it.

His mouth is near my ear. "Ever been eaten out in a closet?"

"Yes. Ours," I whisper, turned on and slightly agitated that he has picked this moment to make advances on me.

Vince holds the shoebox in front of me with one hand and rubs my sensitive spot through my jeans with the other, working his magic. "What about someone else's closet?"

"Vince, not now," I whine.

"I bet there are no microphones in here." His voice is full of lust.

"Babe, I'm trying to work." I have to close my

eyes for a moment because his stimulation is effective.

"I want to taste your pussy."

I press my back against his chest. "I know, but…"

"It'll only take a minute or two." He unbuttons my jeans and then unzips them.

It's highly negligent of me to not call an end to his advances. We have all night for him to eat as much of my pussy as he wants. But gosh, a Vincent Adams orgasm is hard to pass on.

"Damn, you're so wet and hot."

Vince spins me around to face him. He takes the decorative box and my camera out of my hands and sets them on the floor. I let him guide me over to the red velvet bench. He pulls my panties and pants to my ankles. Our steamy gazes connect as he gets on one knee and the other. I swallow the extra moisture in my mouth. This feels so wrong, yet so right.

"No matter how it feels, baby, don't sit," he warns.

I gulp. I can't sit on that bench anyway. I'm too soaking wet to not leave a stain behind.

Vince's moist tongue dives into my slit, probing until it finds what it's looking for.

"Ah," I moan when that silky, wet sensation rounds my clit. His tongue strokes it, and his mouth sucks it. I bet no man knows how to make such an immediate impact the way Vince does. He keeps it going. My legs tremble, and my hands search desperately for something to hold onto. The closest thing I can cling to without damaging anything is the top of Vince's head. My fingers dig into his scalp, but he still doesn't let up.

"I can't..." As I warn him, pleasure sparks in my pussy and expands with each stroke of his tongue.

And he still doesn't let up.

My legs are visibly trembling. "Oh shit..."

His hands clamp down on my ass to keep me stable.

I whimper and moan, fighting hard to control my volume, as pure delight erupts through my lower half. Vince does that thing where he takes it down a notch but stays consistent to make it last at least five seconds longer. When the orgasm ends, I'm satisfied and relieved.

Vince stands. My wobbly legs give out, and he holds me.

"Let's hurry up and get this over with because

it's taking every ounce of willpower to not fuck you right here and right now," he whispers thickly.

I nod vigorously. We kiss. Since he didn't venture past my clit, I can't taste me in his mouth, but I do enjoy the warm wetness of his exerted tongue.

Our tongues circle each other one last time, then we force ourselves to pull apart. Vince takes the box and my camera off the floor and hands them to me. We chuckle as I lift the cardboard lid and return to my mission. *Gosh, he's such a sexy distraction.*

Inside the box are lots of photos of Mita, drinking and eating and posing with friends—none with a child. What kind of mother doesn't have a gang of pictures of her kid?

Vince hands me the box on the tip-top shelf. Inside are her vibrator, handcuffs, tape, three whips, and Kegel balls. "Someone's into kinky shit."

"This is mild compared to what I've found in other marks' hiding places."

Vince sniffs as he smirks. "Remember when I tried BDSM on you?"

I let out a quiet chuckle. "Epic fail."

"Want to try it again?"

I look into his eyes to see if he really means that. He raises his eyebrows twice. He means it.

"Maybe." I wink. We already have the best sex. I thought sex was supposed to take a nosedive after marriage, but for us, it didn't, although we are technically still newlyweds.

"I'm going to hold you to that."

I make my eyes smolder. "Please do."

"Keep that up, and I'm going to throw you on the floor and fuck you right now."

"Well, there's no time for that, so I'll stop." I put the lid on Mita's box.

Vince chuckles as I force my mind back in the game. And then…

"Voilà." I've found a flash drive. I hold it up to show Vince while smiling from ear to ear. The mere fact that Mita stores it way up at the top of her closet says she's keeping secrets.

"Then we're done here?" Vince asks.

"Don't rush me." I hurry to the living room, take my secure tablet out of my bag, and start downloading the files of the flash drive to my computer. It will take three minutes. I return to the bedroom and check between the mattresses for more secrets. I find none. I head to the second bedroom, expecting to see it set up for a child, but instead, I find a full-size bed, two nightstands, and a TV mounted on the wall. There are no toys in the corners, under the bed, or in the closet. And there's no children's clothing in the drawers or hanging up. It's quite baffling. If Mita has a kid, by the looks of it, he doesn't live here. But there was a kid in the house today, and I need his DNA.

I go into the kitchen and rummage through the trash but find nothing definite that I can use. I walk over to the sink and pull out two spoons, a bowl, a glass, and a small plastic cup. I take the cup to my duffel bag and seal it in a sterile plastic bag.

I pose a question to myself: does the child belong to Mita? For sure, the woman we saw leaving the house with the boy was Mita's nanny. Mita's the one who pays her. But there's something off, very off, here. I hurry to the bathroom. Vince is already there. He's holding up a kid's toothbrush and a regular hairbrush.

"Thought you'd be needing these," he whispers in my ear.

I kiss him on the cheek to show my appreciation.

Then I open the cabinet under the sink and find a used razor. All those bathroom items go into sterile bags. Once everything is packed in the duffle, the download finishes. I take the flash drive out of my computer and gesture for Vince to put it back where it came from. He gives me a thumbs-up, takes the drive, and goes.

My phone vibrates in my pocket. I take it out and find a very interesting text from Grey regarding Sir Walter Barnaby that makes me grin from ear to ear.

That was fast, I write back, still happy as a lark.

Just call me lightning man, Grey replies.

Triumphant, I look over at Vince. "We have to get back to the hotel."

CHAPTER EIGHT

"*D*idn't I see you on the airplane?" Mita asked Javar when they ran into each other in the kitchen for lunch.

He studied her face. "I would remember if I saw you."

She blushed. "First class. Seat 3B. You were drinking champagne."

He smirked flirtatiously. "You have a memory on you."

Mita chuckled as though she was sharing an inside joke with herself. "That's because it should've been me."

"Oh, and why is that?"

"Never mind." She touched herself daintily on the chest. "I'm Mita Capelli, and you are…?"

"Bronson Chandler," Javar said. He wanted to pat himself on the back for coming up with such a phallic, fist-pumping, balls-grabbing sort of name on the fly.

"Is nice to meet you, Bronson," she said.

Then, unintentionally, Javar locked eyes with Monroe, who was sitting out on the patio, eating lunch at a table with two men. Javar was relieved that neither man was Charlie Lord. He could tell that Monroe and Charlie shared a special connection—he just didn't know how special. He didn't know much about Charlie other than he was Maggie's cousin, Daisy's husband's brother, and a musician. He was also rich, good looking, and a chick magnet who once liked to party until he dropped. They had a lot in common except that Charlie Lord was into one woman. Javar hadn't made a commitment to monogamy as of yet. Pussy was hard to pass up, and he found Monroe's particularly irresistible.

Actually, he was surprised to see her at the studio that morning. If he'd known about it ahead of time, he probably would've confessed to Maggie that Monroe could be a distraction. He'd first met her after flying from Chicago to LA with Maggie, who brought him to Monroe's Bel-Air estate so they could come up with a plan to clear Jack Lord's name. Jack's rivals had attempted to tarnish his image and create public outcry over his purchase of a popular historical building in Chicago.

One look at Monroe, and Javar knew she was used to men groveling at her feet, mainly because she paid him no mind. There was only one way to play it with a woman like that: pay her no extra special attention. That actually backfired, because she seemed pretty okay with it. However, her nonchalance toward him made Javar want her even more. After that, when he got a little lonely and considered the sort of woman who might make him want to settle down, Monroe Blanco often came to mind. And now they were in the same place together. Javar didn't want to leave LA without spending some quality time with her.

"Excuse me?" Mita dodged her head from side to side, attempting to regain his attention.

His eyes beamed in on hers. "I apologize, love. I thought I saw…" Javar squinted as he looked past her again. He had no idea who the men at the table with Monroe were, but he was hoping Mita would provide the answer.

"Yes, that is Ship Gorman," she said.

Javar smirked. It worked. "Right. I thought so. Are you on his project?"

"Yes, I am. Well, I was. We're over."

"I see... how about we go grab some real lunch, then?"

Mita's expression lit up and then dimmed. "But why are *you* here?"

"I'm working on a project with Gill Blum."

"Oh, yes, Gill."

Javar thought perhaps she was thinking about how strange it was that she saw him on the airplane and then they were in the same studio. Maggie had told him that Mita was sharp and might be slightly paranoid because she'd have a hard time believing that Charlie would do nothing to protect himself. She was probably on edge, waiting for Charlie to make a move. So Javar didn't do anything to make her suspicious.

"But you're right. I have to work. You're so beautiful that I've nearly forgotten."

She lifted a shoulder and pinched it against her chin. "Maybe later we can talk?"

Javar put on his most flirtatious smirk. "I would like that."

"Me too."

They stood smiling at each other. Javar held eye

contact long enough to convince her that he was seriously interested. Once he was sure of it, he took his plate and headed back to the studio. The session was closed, so the door was locked and window shade lowered. Mita wouldn't be able to see him sitting in the back of the control room, chowing down on grilled onion steak wraps and Greek salad while monitoring the spy cameras he'd set up in her room while she was in the studio with Charlie Lord's crew.

Mita had returned to her room, stripped naked, and climbed into bed. Maggie said Mita had a child, but she made no phone calls to anyone. She only checked email on her laptop, smiled at a couple of social-media posts, and then yawned. That signaled the end of computer time. Mita closed her laptop and set it on the desk. She returned to the bed, pulled the comforter over her shoulders, and went to sleep.

Javar would be free for a while. He sent Monroe a text, asking if she was still in the building.

Leaving now, she replied.

All the hairs on the back of Javar's neck stood up. *Wait*, he wrote and looked over at Gill. "Thank you for sharing your space."

Gill waved. "Tell Maggie she can have it anytime."

Javar saluted him and dashed out into the hallway.

His phone vibrated. *No. I'm leaving,* Monroe had texted.

Javar stopped to absorb the message. Once again, Monroe Blanco was rejecting him. But why? He knew when a woman was attracted to him, and she had a classic textbook case of finding him appealing.

She couldn't have gotten that far. *Let's talk,* he texted and then he ran down the hallway, through the foyer, and out the front door.

Javar crossed the lawn and walked down the driveway. He remembered Monroe drove a big black G-Wagen. When he first saw her behind the steering wheel, Javar had thought, *Beautiful vehicle but highly impractical for a single woman like her.* Just like her large estate. The more he got to know Monroe, the more he realized that she did everything big to hide how small she really felt inside. He could identify with that.

Javar made it to the end of the driveway and searched up and down the street. No G-Wagen. His heart dropped as he turned his back on the road and slogged back toward the house. Halfway to the door, his phone buzzed. He quickly flipped it up to look at the screen. It was a response from Monroe.

You're there to work. Charlie's family. Do your best for him, and give me a call when it's over. I like you ;-).

Javar stood still, reading the message over and over. He couldn't stop grinning.

"She likes me."

He shook his fist and skipped the rest of the way to his room. Javar returned to his workspace, realizing he still had a job to do, an obligation to Maggie to fulfill. First, he called Damon, his friend at the Tin Can Club in Hollywood, and made plans to take Mita there that night. After ending the conversation with Damon, Javar decided to get some rest. He hadn't slept in thirty-six hours and was running on fumes. So he turned on the motion detectors in Mita's room. If she moved beyond a radius of two feet from her bed, the alarm would beep. He put on ear buds so that the sound wouldn't project.

He kicked off his shoes, lay on the bed, and thought about the events that had led up to him working for Maggie. He'd first met her in Daisy's condo in Chicago. Before that, he'd spent his days bumming around Europe, Africa, the US, and

South America, partying, exploring, meeting new lovers, and spending what felt like a bottomless trust fund. Life was fun but directionless, and that started to wear on him.

Javar met Champ Davis, the famous Hollywood producer, during a trip to Tenerife. The night Javar told Champ that he was a movie director, he was merely fucking around. He liked to do that—convince famous people he was someone he wasn't, just to see what he could get out of them. They were both coked out and drunk. Javar barely remembered they'd socialized at all, but two days later, Champ Davis called and asked if he wanted to fly to New York to direct a new TV pilot about three high-powered female lawyers looking for love in the big city. He had nothing else to do that day, so he said, "Sure!"

To Javar's amazement, he managed to bullshit his way to success. The pilot got picked up, and he was asked to direct the show. But he hated the hours and the work involved in making TV. He called Dexter Frampton, his sister's husband's brother, to ask if he was interested. Dexter was a producer, not a director, so he turned down the project.

However, Dexter mentioned that he was looking to produce a travel show, and Javar immediately thought of Daisy Blanchard. She'd been an award-winning travel writer before she became saddled with that billionaire asshole, Charlie's brother. Javar heard that Daisy and her husband had separated—it was reported by all the tabloids. She was single again, and he wanted another shot at her. So he did what he did best—he convinced Dexter to make him the director of the show by working for free as long as he based the program on Daisy's book.

Dexter didn't agree right away. He needed to read the book first and then get back to Javar with an answer. Javar didn't even know the title of the book. He wanted the one woman who consistently told him no, and a door had finally opened for him to get his chance at having her. Dexter eventually found the book on his own, read it, and loved it. Long story short, Dexter agreed to Javar's terms. Longer story shorter, Daisy got sick and couldn't fly to France to shoot the first group of shows. So Javar went to France and found her in a state far worse than he could've guessed. Then Maggie and Daisy's sister, Angelina, showed up with doctors, who carted Daisy away. It all happened fast, and he gathered right away that Maggie wouldn't be easily opposed. If he wanted to learn more about what was going on, he would have to schmooze her.

Of course, Maggie questioned whether his intentions were good. But he convinced her he would never do anything to hurt Daisy—he loved her too much. Maggie searched his eyes for what felt like an uncomfortable five minutes. Then she said, "You're a good-looking guy. I could use you." And that was exactly what she did.

He was standing in the kitchen with Maggie when the news teaser aired. "How Jack Lord's bid to own one of the most prestigious landmarks in Chicago is tied to his questionable past…" It all happened quickly after that. Maggie set out to clear Jack's name, and Javar had ditched Dexter's show to help her.

He had been working off and on with Maggie for over a year. Monroe usually kept her distance. He guessed she was standoffish because she was afraid of their chemistry. Once, when he showed up early for a meeting, he overheard Maggie say, "What about Javar? Fuck handsome—the guy is abnormally beautiful."

"But toxic," Monroe was quick to say. "And I'm done with toxic men, even the abnormally beautiful ones—unless they're clients. That way I know there are boundaries that can't be crossed."

"Then it's yourself you can't trust?" Maggie had asked her.

"Bingo."

Javar stood outside Maggie's door, thinking. His emotions shifted from excited and confident about seducing Monroe to ashamed of himself for wanting to break her resolve. So he decided to back off. He was thankful to have made that choice because they had become friends, even if he couldn't keep his heart from skipping a beat whenever she was near.

Lying on his bed at the studio, he knew one thing for sure—he wanted Monroe Blanco and was tired of waiting to have her. Javar closed his eyes, comforted by his resolve to make something happen between them. Six hours later, he was woken up by the alarm's beep. He sat up and shook off the exhaustion.

"Showtime," he muttered.

Mita was on the move.

CHAPTER NINE

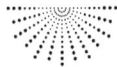

CHARLIE LORD

*F*inishing the project didn't take as long as I thought it would. There was no time for fuckups. The entire crew felt the pressure, including Ship. We were focused, sharp. By 4:55 p.m., Mita and Fidel's parts had been recorded. By 6:54 p.m., we had mixed them into the final recording and finished laying the entire soundtrack for the film. It took us another hour and forty-five minutes to view the film, making sure there were no mistakes. There were none.

After leaving the studio, I rushed home, packed my suitcase, and caught a cab to the airport. Now it's eleven thirty at night, and I'm sitting in my private jet on a direct flight from LA to Paris. It will take a long eleven hours to get there.

I spoke to Maggie briefly on my way home from the studio. She said she had some information to share, but it was five in the morning, and she and Vince had arrived in Zurich late.

"Zurich?" I said.

"Long story. I'll catch you up later. I promise."

And that was the end of the call.

Chloe, one of the flight attendants, walks by to make sure I'm buckled in. I give her a thumbs-up, and she returns the gesture. I like Chloe. She makes me comfortable. She's a young and beautiful woman, works just about every private flight I take, but has never directly or subtly flirted with me. Women like her don't usually behave that way, in my experience, and her not coming on to me makes it easy to relax on an eleven-hour flight.

Rex, the pilot, announces it's time for takeoff. I hold onto the arm of my seat and wait. One, two, three... the jet speeds down the runway, and soon we have liftoff. The countdown has begun. Every mile of thousands brings me closer to the one woman I can't live without.

PARIS, FRANCE - 9:03 P.M.

. . .

I WAKE UP JUST IN TIME TO TAKE IN THE LIGHTS below. Paris is an exciting city. I call it a consummate virgin because no matter how many times I'm here, it always feels like the first time. Before disembarking, I say good-bye to the captains and crew. There wasn't much interaction because I was out for most of the flight. My mind and body are energized, at least until I remember my fucking woes. Mita is blackmailing me, and if I don't give her what she wants, she could destroy my relationship with the only woman I can ever love. Worry returns, and the need to see Angelina grips me.

As soon as I'm off the airplane, a car is ready to take me to the city center, which is about a half an hour from Paris Le Bourget airport. On the ride to the hospital, I call Angel and let her know I'm on my way. She's excited and says she'll meet me out front. It looks as if I'm going to reach her before any bad news can. The car dips and turns down familiar streets. The city can look deceptively charming. Once, when I was walking through Lafayette Park on my way to the train station, two guys attempted to rob me at knifepoint.

"Are you serious?" I asked, making sure they were dedicated to the process.

They looked at each other, perhaps taking into account that I was American. The guy asked me again to give him my wallet.

"I'm one of those violent fucking cowboys you don't want to fuck with," I said to give them a bit more information to chew on. The one thing my dad did right was make me take karate from the age of five until I was fifteen. Speaking French, one guy told the other that I must think I'm John Wayne. They laughed. They said, "Let's gut John Wayne."

One of them tried to stab me in the gut while the other went for my face. The rule in karate is to follow the assault. I went into automatic pilot, and after my defensive moves were complete, they stood disarmed and facing me. John Wayne was waiting for them to make their next move. I could've easily hurt them very badly, but offense is not the guiding principle of karate. The guys were smart and ran away. I was relieved that I didn't have to send two bad kids to the hospital that day. However, from that moment on, I knew how gritty the city could be. It behooved me to be on the alert. Visitors could easily get lost in the charm, the smell and taste of food, the old cobblestone streets, and centuries-old architecture. But I have learned the hard way not to be dazzled by any of it. As in all other big cities in the world, I never let my guard down.

THE CAR FINALLY ARRIVES AT THE HOSPITAL IN THE 10th Arrondissement. The facility looks like a cross between an eighteenth-century castle and a prison. I tip the driver and thank him for the ride.

"You call if need service," my driver says.

"Thanks, I will." I step out on the sidewalk in front of a green courtyard. It's late, but there's lots of foot traffic on the sidewalks. Angel said she'd be waiting out front, but I don't see her. I take out my phone.

"Charlie!"

I look up to see Angel running in my direction. It's like she's in slow motion. I've never been so damn happy to see her. She jumps into my arms. I hoist her off the ground, and she wraps her legs around me as we kiss. The familiar taste of her mouth makes my head spin. Her body is so soft and warm. Magnetic energy flows from her heart to mine, proving to me for the millionth time that I'm in love.

Angel forces her mouth off mine and squeezes me tightly. "Gosh, I missed you, Charlie. You smell so good."

"You do too." I kiss her again deeply.

"Angelina, we should go," a guy with a French accent says.

We stop kissing, and about ten feet away, there's a dark-haired guy smoking a cigarette with one hand shoved in his pocket. Angel jumps off me and grabs my hand. "Oh, I want you to finally meet Anton." She drags me to the grimacing guy.

I narrow my eyes to get a better look at this Anton. I've heard about him. He visited Daisy and Jack in Martha's Vineyard once or maybe twice. He called to see whether Angel would be there, but she was either dancing in a show or we were on vacation, surfing in Panama. If memory serves me correctly, he's Daisy's cousin on her mother Heloise's side of the family. He's not a blood relative of Angel's, which might explain why he's glaring at me as if he wants to skin me alive.

"Charlie, Anton. Anton, Charlie," Angelina says when we reach him.

Finally, he gives a forced grin like he's making himself do it for her sake. "The infamous Charlie Lord."

I narrow my eyes, wondering what the fuck he means by *infamous*. I shake his hand, keeping my thoughts to myself, and turn to Angel. "How's Jacques?"

"I heard he's doing better. I haven't been able to see him because they all got here before I did and drove the staff crazy."

"Who's here?"

"My uncles…" Her eyes expand. "And Heloise, Daisy's mother." She sighs. "Also Daisy and Jack. It was the type-A reunion all the way."

"Well, why are we leaving? We should see Jacques as soon as we can."

"Visiting is over," Anton says.

I glare at him. I don't like his fucking tone.

Angel hangs onto my arm. "The good news is that he's going to be discharged in the morning. Daisy and Jack are going to fly him to Bordeaux."

"So soon?" I ask.

"Papa insists on leaving. He's stubborn. That's why he's here in the first place." Angel looks off with watery eyes. "He would've died if it weren't for Madeleine."

I rub her back consolingly, and Anton watches as if I've just violated my own girlfriend. This guy definitely has a problem with me being here. Actually, I sort of remember Angel saying that they used to "hang out." Now I want to know what the hell she meant by that.

Anton checks his watch. "We must go, or we will miss the flight."

I frown, confused. "Flight?"

"We're flying to Bordeaux tonight," Angel says. "Everyone else will be there in the morning. Daphne has arranged for in-home care for Papa at Mes Fleurs with doctors, nurses, and the works. I want to arrive early to make sure everything goes smoothly when he arrives. I mean, because you know how he is."

I'm pretty sure Jacques is a difficult patient. Once, he plugged in an amplifier and it short-circuited. The electric current knocked him out, and we insisted he go to the hospital. But he refused to go, and there was no getting him to change his mind. He said he didn't like hospitals because that was where people went to die, and he had more lives than a cat, so hospitals weren't the place for a man like himself.

I take my phone out of the pocket of my pants, and Angelina gasps.

"Charlie, you're not supposed to keep your phone there."

"Sorry, babe, I wasn't thinking." Angel believes that radio waves are harmful to our health. "My pilot and crew can fly us to Bordeaux."

"I have the tickets already," Anton says.

This guy's attitude... "I can pay you back for them if you need the money."

He sniffs bitterly. "I don't need your money."

Part of me wants to take his head off, but Angel looks confused by our interaction.

"My pilot will take us. You can come along if you want." I finish placing the call and turn my back on Anton.

He tells Angel, in French, that he'll see her at the vineyard and that he's had his fill of rich Americans who throw their money around. Angel tries to talk him into coming with us, arguing that my jet will be more comfortable and safe and everyone knows the airplanes in Europe aren't the best. Anton flat out refuses her offer. I look at the concrete when he kisses her good-bye. It sounds like he's kissing her lips. I'm fuming at the thought of it. But when I look up, Angelina's bright eyes are smiling at me.

"I'm glad you were able to come tonight," she says.

"Me too."

We kiss, and I squeeze two handfuls of her ass and nail her pussy against my burgeoning hard-on. I wish her tight black pants weren't separating my skin from her skin. Anton's bad attitude is in the distance, and my lust for Angel has ignited. We're going to be the only two on the flight. Soon, we'll be joining the mile-high club.

I CALL THE DRIVER WHO DROPPED ME OFF, AND HE takes us back to the airport. Angel and I go straight to the airplane from the terminal, and she sits beside me as we wait to taxi to the runway and take off. I've already instructed the flight attendants to not come into the cabin unless we call them. We don't want drinks. We don't want food. I want to dine on my Angel.

"So why is Anton being such an asshole? Rich Americans?"

Angelina sighs. "I don't know. He just broke up with his girlfriend, so he's not doing so well. That's probably why he's so crabby."

"But he kissed you…" The question I want to ask is on the tip of my tongue.

Angelina pats my thigh. "Charlie, don't be jealous. Anton and I are not having an affair."

"But you had one in the past, right?"

She closes her eyes and sighs gravely. "Okay, yes, we did, but we were younger, and I wasn't in love with you yet."

"Is he still in love with you?"

"No," she says as if she's sure of her answer.

"Then what's his fucking problem?"

"I don't know. I think it's just a bad breakup. He'll be fine in a few days. Anton doesn't stay sour for long."

For some reason, I can't stop feeling that his *sourness* is personal and has everything to do with him wanting my fiancée.

My fiancée… Angel and I have never set a date for our wedding. Maybe we should. I'm positive that only by death do I want us to part, and I want that to happen many, many years from now.

I turn to look at her, and she yawns.

"I'm pretty sure leaving the show to come here was the right move. Was it?" She looks at me with a conflicted expression.

I shrug. "I don't know. Only you can answer that." I don't know why I feel butt hurt that this is what she's thinking about at a time when I'm ready to suggest setting a wedding date. Maybe she's been the reason for the delay. When I asked Angelina to marry me, she took forever to give me an answer—at least thirty seconds. I even got up off my knee and told her to forget I ever asked. And then out of nowhere, she said, "Yes." That word was music to my ears, but I should've questioned why it took her so long to say it.

Suddenly, I don't want to join the mile-high club anymore. I take my arm from around her and lean closer to the window. She yawns again. Hell, maybe she's inadvertently telling me she's too tired to have sex. Maybe it's time for me to read between the fucking lines. Maybe I'm more in love with her than she is with me.

The captain announces we're about to take off. Angel and I look straight ahead as the airplane bolts down the runway and lifts off. Once we're in the air, I can't help but think about Anton and his shitty attitude. I think he knows Angel is into him and that she's never going to marry me. I'm in his fucking way.

"Charlie?"

I shift suddenly in my seat. "Yeah."

"Um…" She unclips her seatbelt, undoes the

button of my pants, and unzips them. "I want you inside me."

My heart thumps a mile a minute. Like a racing avalanche, lust rushes back into my body.

Her finger rounds the tip of my dick. She does this with the skill of a *Kama Sutra* aficionado.

I lick my bottom lip and moan because her hot, wet mouth now covers the tip of my dick. Her mouth slides up and down my shaft and rounds my head.

I put my hand under her chin to stop her from taking more of me in. "I don't want to come yet, baby."

"I don't want you to either." Angelina has fire in her eyes as she stands and pulls her pants down. She entrances me with her hips and pussy then rotates her body and gives me an ass to salivate over.

I hold my hands out. "Sit on it."

She smirks naughtily at my erection. Slowly, she moves toward me as if she's teasing me. Angel straddles me. Her pussy is right in front of my face, and I want to grab it and suck on it just as much as I want to be inside her. So now I'm delirious.

She inches her wet delightfulness closer to my cock. I shift my hips up so we can make contact faster than the pace she's going. Suddenly, Angel straightens her legs and takes her wetness far away from me.

"What?" I say, frustrated.

She puts her finger across her lips, telling me to stay quiet. I take a deep breath to try to settle my excitement. The anticipation is swirling through my dick. I'm trapped in a daze that I can't escape.

Gradually, she drops her pussy toward my lap. It takes willpower not to just slam it over my dick and bang the shit out of her. I close my eyes and wait. Patience is a virtue. First, the tip of my cock is sucked into her hot wetness. Now that I've conquered one barrier that wants to slay me, I have to contend with her tightness. Angel is so fucking tight. I can feel every inch of her insides. Up and down, she bobs on my dick. I'm thankful that she's taking it slow. That's because she knows if she goes too fast, I'll explode.

"You like it, baby." She sighs.

I nod wildly. "Fuck." The blood is rushing through my dick. It won't be long now.

"Tell me when to stop."

My eyes are closed and head pinned against her sternum. There's no way I can tell her to stop. She's going to have to read the signs. She's familiar with them.

"Shit," I mutter and grab her hips and pin her against my dick. If she shifts one more time, I'm coming. But Angel hardly ever plays fair when she's horny. She circles her hips and tightens her pussy around my dick. That's it. I see white as I let loose inside her.

I shout, losing my mind.

Angel's hand comes over my mouth, but she doesn't stop twisting her hips. When my orgasm ends, I hug her close to me. I'm pretty sure she lives to slay me with her pussy. But I also like to do some slaying of my own. I carefully guide her down on the carpeted floor between the seats, spread her legs, and cover her clit with my mouth. I want her to come, and come hard. The trick is to not fuck around. I stay in one spot and stimulate the fuck out of that area. Angel tries twisting her lower half as she whimpers and rubs my scalp. There's no way she's getting away from my mouth. It doesn't take long for her to cry out. But I don't stop. I keep going until I lose count of how many times she shakes, shivers, and screams.

Finally, she lies back, limp, and I lie down beside her.

"Wow, I can sleep for days now," she says.

"Let's just get married." Shit. That slipped out.

She turns her gaze on me and blinks once and then twice. "Okay."

I sit up. "What? Really?"

"Yeah, I mean…" She sits up. "After being in that hospital today, watching everybody but Madeleine make decisions for my father, I realized something. If anything like that happens to you, I'm the one who knows you best. Plus…"

"I told you that if I die, I want my ashes spread across the Mediterranean Sea. But you know would Jack would do instead?"

"What?" She sounds really curious.

"Have Reverend Weasel preside over my funeral and then bury my rotting corpse in a box and plant me six feet underground."

"Exactly. And do you know what Daisy would do to me?"

"What?"

"Something similar."

We chuckle.

"But you would rather be cremated and have your ashes dropped on the Himalayas," I say.

"I did want that, but now I think I want to join you in the Mediterranean."

I laugh. No one makes me laugh like Angel. "Then that's the plan."

"But truthfully, if I asked Daisy to spread my ashes in the Mediterranean, she would do it."

A picture of my brother comes to mind. "Jack would do the same for me. If I asked."

"But still… I want to be your wife, Charlie. I want to be all yours, and I want you to be mine."

I never thought I would hear her say that. I guide her on top of me, and we lie in the middle of the aisle, kissing, rubbing, and hugging each other until the pilot announces that the airplane will land in ten minutes.

CHAPTER TEN

MAGGIE ADAMS

*O*n the way back to the hotel yesterday, Grey bent my ear with another update. The nanny had taken the child to the 7th Arrondissement to a luxury apartment owned by Ralph McIntyre, a famous pianist. However, since Ralph wasn't home, his sister Laura McIntyre had taken custody of the child. Ms. McIntyre is from Boston, Massachusetts. She's in Paris to visit her nephew.

The child's name is Abel, and he's two and a half years old. Grey was able to learn all the details we needed because Laura spent the afternoon on the phone with lawyers in the US and Paris, trying to work out a custody arrangement for Abel. She told the lawyers that Mita is the mother and Ralph is the father, although she referred to Mita spitefully as "that Italian girl." Ralph isn't known to have any children. He's fifty-four, but Rosalie, his thirty-two-year-old wife, is currently pregnant. Laura, who's fifty-six, wants to gain full custody of Abel without exposing her brother's infidelity.

When we made it back to the hotel, Vince quickly dealt with some A&Rt Media business. Gray allowed me to listen to recordings of Laura's conversations with the lawyers while waiting for the lab results. Laura's tone set off an alarm within me. She sounded desperate enough to smuggle Abel out of the country, and actually, I was pretty okay with that. The farther he was from Mita's clutches, the better. Then the lab results came back, bringing alarming news. I called Jack and asked that he use his special resources to put a security detail on Laura. This situation is very much in flux, and I have a proposition that it would behoove Sir Walter Barnaby to accept.

Now we're riding through the rolling green hills of Zurich on our way to Sir Walter Barnaby's estate. I called him yesterday and told him that we should discuss Abel man to woman. The line went dead. So I called back and left a message. My words were simple. "You're the father. Let's discuss, or I'll be forced to come clean about it," and gave him my phone number.

Sir Walter called right back, and now we're here. Our driver navigates the car up the winding road. Healthy evergreens and lush grasslands surround us. Vince and I swoon over the majestic lake and stony mountain we just passed. The pressure that I felt yesterday is off. I have what I need, and now it's time to force Mita into checkmate.

The car turns and stops in front of a big iron gate. The driver keys in the code Sir Walter Barnaby gave me. The keypad beeps, and gates part. Evergreens run thick along the private drive.

Vince stares deep into the tree line. "I have a funny feeling about this place."

I look out the window on my side. "Don't worry. We'll be fine."

When I turn, Vince is already facing me and wearing a very curious expression. "You sound sure of it. But I'm not."

I look down at his hand and fold my fingers between his. "Trust me?"

Suddenly, we're out of the trees. The road

zigzags through more emerald-green grass as we head toward the large modern house with sharp edges and a lot of glass.

"What if I weren't here with you, and you got into a dangerous situation. How would you handle it?"

I sigh forcefully and shift my body to face him. He's just not going to ease up on being worried someone's going to take my head off. "Listen, babe, I'm trained."

He shakes his head as if he's confused by my words. "Trained to do what?"

"To fight."

He frowns as if I'm speaking Martian, but I don't let my serious expression dissolve.

"I've never even seen you make a fist, Mags," he says as if hurling an accusation.

The car drives along the roundabout and parks near a red-clay cobblestone walkway.

"I've been in training intensely ever since we returned from our honeymoon."

"Fighting?"

I shrug nonchalantly. "Hand-to-hand combat as well as speed, agility, and endurance."

Vince swipes his hand down his face, squeezing like he does when he's frustrated. "Why am I just now hearing this? And aren't you working for Jack mostly?"

"Yeah."

"Why the hell does he need you to learn how to fight and carry a gun?"

"He doesn't."

"But you didn't need to know how to fight or carry a weapon before you started working for him."

I shift uncomfortably in my seat. "The gun and fighting skills are just instruments that I'll use if I need them, but more than likely, I won't."

Vince's frown deepens. "Huh?"

I sigh and rub my scalp, trying to calm myself, hoping that the energy inside me spills over into him.

"I'm trained."

"If what you're doing is safe, then why do you need a gun?"

I open my mouth to defend my position, but I'm at a loss for words. The question is valid, and the answer will just validate all of his fears. So I reach forward and pat the driver on the shoulder. "Vince. This is Lian."

Vince looks even more confused and unhappy.

The brawny blond guy turns to the side but not

all the way around to look at us.

"Lian, could you please lower the screen?" I say.

A screen lowers beneath the rearview mirror.

I tap my pearl stud. "Notice I wore these today?"

"Not really, but yeah. You don't wear earrings."

I smile, happy Vince is engaging. "So look at the screen."

The screen shows a picture of Vince and me in the back seat.

Vince's glare bops back and forth from the image of us to the back of Lian's head. I never revealed that I knew the driver because I was hoping I wouldn't have to. Finally, he shakes his head as if he still doesn't like one part of what he just learned.

"I just don't want to lose you, babe."

I take his hand. "You won't. I promise."

"There's no way you can make that promise if you're carrying a gun. Do you know how to use it?"

"Yes." I press my lips together to show him I mean what I say.

"I still don't think…"

"Babe, can we talk about it later? We have to go inside."

He blinks at me with a blank expression. "Okay,

whatever."

I feel burdened by Vince's extreme, but legitimate, reaction to what he just learned about my new career choice. Half of me thinks he's behaving this way because he wants me safely back at A&Rt Media, and the other half grasps his concern. Vince slides out of the back seat on my side. We stand facing each other, gazing at each other, speaking without words.

"I love you," he finally says.

"I love you too."

We kiss tenderly, link arms, and walk over a bridge, which straddles a narrow canal that runs through the property. We make it to the other side of the bridge, head up a crystal stone walkway, and stop in front of a giant frosted-glass door. I show Vince one last tight smile of assurance. He gives me the same smile with a nod. I'm relaxed enough to ring the doorbell, and it chimes and is opened by a silver-haired gentleman in a light-blue button-down shirt and white linen pants. I recognize him immediately.

He nods once. "You are Ms. Adams?" he says in a thick British accent.

His hands are behind his back, which clues me in that we will not be shaking hands. So I straighten my posture and thumb over at Vince. "Yes. Sir Walter Barnaby, this is my husband, Vince."

He studies Vince scrupulously. Then what I hoped would happen occurs: Vince reaches out to shake Sir Walter Barnaby's hand. Barnaby hesitates —the pause is so quick that you'd have to be looking for it to notice it—but he responds to Vince's gesture. I make sure my hands stay pinned to my sides.

"We should get right to it," I say.

"Please, come in." Barnaby steps back so we can enter.

Vince and I follow him down a sterile-white marble hallway with a high ceiling. Its glass walls show a view of a wide lake nestled against a grassy, rocky mountain. It's afternoon, so dipping sunrays glide across the surface of the water. I want to compliment Barnaby on his beautiful home, but it would cause me to lose the edge I gained the second he shook Vince's hand after refusing to shake mine.

We make it to a spacious room with more high windows, large, angular, modern furniture, and a big white leather chair for Barnaby to sit in and regain the power. If Vince weren't here, I would tell Barnaby that I prefer to stand. Jack taught me to never give up the position of power in these sorts of situations. It's the only way to tell if the other person is sweating. "Remember this. If a person is cool, calm, and collected, then you should be on guard," Jack said. I already knew why. A confident person, depending on the situation, has reliable protection in place—it could be a gun, guards, or the solid upper hand. Sir Walter Barnaby crosses his legs as he sits back in his chair, but he shifts twice before settling into a comfortable position. He's nervous, and that's a good thing.

Though sitting, I set my feet wide and lean toward the man of the house, resting my elbows on my thighs. "The child you gave Mita Capelli—she's using him to blackmail someone very close to me, and a second man as well."

Barnaby's composed expression shifts from my face to Vince's and then back to me. "I don't know what you're talking about."

I unlatch my handbag. The rule is to never carry a bag that looks large enough to hold a weapon. My purse is small, which is why Barnaby doesn't flinch when I open it and take out a neatly folded, two-page report. I calmly rise to my feet and walk the report to him. It takes him a moment, but he finally takes the pages, unfolds them, and reads.

I walk back to the sofa and sit closer to Vince.

"You're the father, and Mita Capelli is not the mother of the child, but you've been paying her through Le Grande Symphony to keep Abel and protect your secret." I lean forward. "Now, I don't give a fuck why you're paying Mita to play mom to the child you had with Ariel Hampton, but she's crossed lines." I tell him about Ralph McIntyre, who has also been paying her because he believes the child is his.

Barnaby's skin has turned red. "Who else knows?"

My heart sinks. That's the one question I didn't want to hear him ask. I rise to my feet. "The right people, Sir Walter Barnaby." I tap Vince on the shoulder, cuing him in to stand when I do. He does. Two big guys walk into the room, blocking the way out. One of them asks in Dutch if everything's okay.

"As long as you don't start a fight. I promise that you won't get very far," I say in Dutch. Of course, I'm only half bluffing. I don't want anyone to get hurt, but right now Lian should be in position with a weapon aimed at one of the guys. My weapon is strapped to my ankle. I've been trained on an effective drop-roll-and-retrieve maneuver, so I'll be able to get my shot off on the other guy.

Vince sets his shocked look on me. I'm slightly concerned by how he's processing this situation and praying that it deescalates fast.

Finally, Sir Walter Barnaby rises to his feet. "We are fine," he says to his goons.

They scowl at me, then turn and walk out of the room.

"Houseguests?" I ask.

Barnaby smirks at Vince. "Your wife is a tough lady."

"Yes. She is."

Barnaby studies me. Then he grunts as though he's just thought of something amusing. "I promise you, I didn't know anything about what Mita was doing to the others."

"She's doing it for money. You must not be paying enough," I say.

He narrows his eyes as if my response bothers him. "I will handle her."

"How?"

Barnaby folds his arms. "That is not your concern."

"If she ends up dead, I'm coming after you."

I can feel Vince tense up beside me.

"I'm not a murderer, Mrs. Adams."

I doubt that very much, but I keep my comment

to myself. "I have a better suggestion for you, Sir Walter."

I wait until he gives me the look that says he's ready to hear it.

TWENTY MINUTES LATER

Vince and I are back in the car. He's been quiet from the moment we got in. I'm letting him have the silence to process what just happened.

"Was that your plan all along?" he finally asks.

"Yes, it was."

"So now Sir Walter Barnaby is your client?" He sounds as if he's still trying to wrap his mind around it.

I grin big. "Yes, he is, and as you've heard, he's going to come clean about having a child out of wedlock with Ariel Hampton. We're going to say that the child has been in the care of a nanny— which he has—and Mita's going to keep her damn mouth closed so she doesn't go to jail for fraud and extortion." I look Vince directly in the eyes. "And believe me, she will go to jail."

After holding my gaze for a number of seconds,

Vince sighs. "Damn it, Maggie. I'm scared for you, but you've also impressed me. To tell you the truth, I was turned on back there."

I chuckle in relief. "So was I. You responded right on cue. You know, we can do this together."

"What?" he says as though he can hardly believe what I suggested. But there's something about his hint of a smile that tells me he's intrigued. "Babe, I run a multibillion-dollar media corporation."

I could argue a different point, which is that he owns A&Rt Media and can pay very smart people to run it, but I want the idea of changing careers to sit with Vince a little longer before I say anything else.

"It sure would be fun working together like this, wouldn't it?" I say to give him more information to add to this think bank.

"Right," he manages to say. "So where to next?"

"LA. I owe Mita Capelli a talking-to."

Vince flexes his eyebrows as though he likes the sound of that. I wink at him. He's into my world, and holy hell, do I love it. But first I call Charlie and update him.

CHAPTER ELEVEN

CHARLIE LORD

We're at the Mes Fleurs Vineyard, and it's noon. Jack and Daisy have already flown Jacques in. A team of nurses and his local doctor are here. So is Daisy's insane mother, Heloise. The last I saw, she was in the hallway ordering the maid to put fresh new linens on all the beds. I was surprised that Daisy came behind her and ordered her mother to go to her room or find something recreational to do but to stop fucking with the staff. Daisy actually said "fucking." It made me want to stand up straight and clap. Heloise did respond, but just then, Maggie called my phone. I stepped out of the house and walked to the back, near the small cottages, for privacy.

Now I shake my head. I can hardly believe what

Maggie just told me. I knew Mita Capelli was a special kind of crazy, but wow. I never knew she was that far out.

"So I'm off the hook?"

"Just keep your dick out of seriously crazy chicks, and you'll be just fine," Maggie says.

I rub my forehead, still unable to believe it. "But really, the kid is not even hers? I heard she was pregnant for nine months."

"They do sell prosthetic bellies."

"And she was blackmailing David McIntyre?"

"Yep. You would be the second baby-daddy." She laughs at her own comment.

It's sort of tragically funny, so I laugh a little too. "And this Sir Walter Barnaby's coming clean about the child?"

"That's right. And I'm his new publicist-slash-fixer."

I smirk. "He's smart to hire you. Shit, Maggie, when did you become so good at this shit?"

"I don't know. It just sort of happened. But listen, I'm on my way to break the hard truth to crazy lady. Don't relax yet because she can still blow up your life. My suggestion is that you do what Sir Walter Barnaby is doing."

At first I draw a blank, but then I remember the

approach Maggie's having him take. "Tell the truth?"

"It shall set you free, Charlie."

I close my eyes and swallow the knot of dread that's stuck in my throat. I take a few steps to stand on the grassy hill. Down below are rows of grapevines stretched across the valley. It sure is a sight for sore eyes.

"Yeah... it will literally set me free," I say.

"You know what? I'm not going to argue with you, Charlie. Just think about it."

"I didn't think we were heading down the road of having an argument."

"Listen, I have to go," Maggie says.

"Oh, wait. I wanted to tell you that Angel and I are just going to do it."

"Do what?"

The words come to my mind first, and now I have to force them out of my mouth. "Get married."

She grunts facetiously. "So is that your plan? Marry her so if she finds out the truth, she can't leave you so easily?"

"Huh? No," I say as though offended, but the truth is that's a large part of my strategy.

"Charlie, you can act like an idiot sometimes.

But you're not an idiot, so…"

I look behind me because I need to sit. On the porch, two cottages away, stands Anton, smoking a cigarette and watching me as if he's heard our entire conversation.

"All right. Talk to you soon, Mags."

"Good-bye," she says briskly and ends the call.

Great. Now she's pissed at me for not doing what she suggested, which would be love suicide.

"Your call sound serious," Anton says.

I don't like the accusation in his voice. "It's my cousin, Maggie."

"Maggie?"

I'm surprised he knows her. "Yeah."

He walks down the steps. "How is she?"

I narrow an eye at him. Is he to be trusted? "She's fine, I guess."

He nods and offers me a cigarette. I shake my head. "I quit a long time ago."

"Ha. Angelina does not like cigarettes."

I chuckle. "That's why I quit."

"She's very convincing, no?"

Again, I hesitate, wondering if getting into a conversation with this guy is safe.

"Tonight there is a party. Would you like to come? Of course, you bring Angelina."

"So what's your angle?" I ask without thinking.

He tilts his head. "Angle?"

Since I let the cat out of the bag, I might as well release the lion too. "Are you still in love with my fiancée?"

Anton freezes before he puts the cigarette between his lips. "Fiancée? You're getting married."

"Yeah. Soon." My tone is brasher than I like.

"Angelina wears no ring?"

It takes me a second to determine that he's asked me a question. "She doesn't believe in it."

He nods thoughtfully and then snickers. "No, she does not."

I don't like the way he's insinuating that he knows her just as well as I do.

"So we go to the party tonight? We drink. We dance. We have fun," he says.

For some reason, I feel as if going to that party is like letting a fox into our chicken coop. "I don't know. I'll have to ask Angel. She may want to stay close to Jacques."

Anton looks at me scrupulously as he takes a drag of his cigarette. "You do not want to hang out with me?"

I shake my head. "No. What do I have against you?"

"I do not know." He's got this tiny smile. "But ask Angel if she wants to come, and let me know what she says."

A knot forms in my chest. "I will," I say, contemplating whether I should really say something. "Later."

Anton snorts as I turn my back on him. The conversation leaves me fuming. He and I are never going to be good. I make it back into the main house in time to catch Angel heading up the tower steps.

"Where are you going?" I ask although I know good and well where she's going.

"To see Papa."

"But he said he wants to rest."

"I don't care." She looks at me with seductive doe eyes. "Are you coming?"

What the hell does she expect me to say when she has a face like that? "Okay, but first…" I hold her and guide her back against the wall.

"Down, boy," she whispers in my ear.

She says that because I'm hard. I kiss her parted lips, and she responds graciously. I can tell that her body's not in it. She's too anxious to see Jacques.

She wiggles out of my embrace and takes my

hand. "Come on. I don't want Heloise walking by and questioning me."

We rush up the stairs.

"Hey," I say.

Angel doesn't stop moving upward. "What?"

I open my mouth and then close it.

She glances back at me. "What is it?"

"Nothing." I was going to tell her about Anton's invitation, but now isn't the time.

"Okay."

We reach the top. Classical music is playing softly throughout the North Tower wing. Lots of light flows through hallways, and there's a pleasant scent in the air. It's floral but not too sweet. Our steps have slowed down. Angel is in seek-and-find mode as she looks inside each room we pass. I keep my gaze fastened to the back of her head, haunted by Maggie's suggestion. Should I tell Angel the truth about the small number of seconds I had my dick inside Mita? The mistake was supposed to be inconsequential and never to be mentioned again, but here it is, tearing a gaping hole into my ass.

We arrive at the threshold of Jacques's room. He stands in front of the large window with his back to us. He's wearing crisp navy-blue pajamas that seem to swallow his narrow frame.

"Papa?" Angel calls timidly.

Jacques turns. His face lights up. "Ma fleur, Charles," he says in a tone I've come to really like to hear. I wish my own dad had spoken to me that way when I walked into the room. Charles Lord was hard, unloving, demanding, and cold. Until this day, I haven't cried over his death. And I don't think Jack has, either. But if anything happens to Jacques, my heart would break into a trillion pieces. I love him as if he's my own father, and in a lot of ways, he is.

Angel runs toward him and then stops. "Is it safe?"

He opens his arms and waves her toward him. "Come here."

She finishes her course and hugs him and kisses him on both cheeks. "You don't have a fever."

"I bounce back fast."

I'm next to give him a big hug. "Glad you're up."

"Can't much keep me down," he says with a chuckle. "Let's go sit."

We follow Jacques through the stone archway and out the glass door to the outside patio. Bushels of pink rose plants are aligned throughout the space, making it look as if we're in a garden. We sit in three of the four big armchairs with matching ottomans, facing the rolling green hills, the valley of grape vines and narrow, snaking lakes, and—far to the east and west—the tops of two castles.

"Did you finish the project?" Jacques asks me.

I knew he would. I smile, satisfied, and nod. "Yes, I did."

He pumps his fists in celebration. "I knew you would. How did it go?"

"Papa, you're not supposed to talk about work," Angel says.

"One answer is all I need, and then I'm done."

"Everybody's happy," I say.

Jacques relaxes even more in his chair as he closes his eyes. "That sun sure feels good."

Soft, warm breezes glide gently through the air. I've never seen Jacques sunbathe. It's almost like watching a roadrunner sleeping in a nest.

"So what are you going to do differently, Papa?" Angel asks.

Jacques takes a long sigh. "God doesn't have to tell me more than twice. I'll slow down. I've been thinking about retiring."

Angel scoots to the edge of her seat. "Twice?"

Jacques quickly opens his eyes. I can tell he

didn't mean to say that. "I've had a scare with my heart before."

Her mouth falls open, and she looks at Jacques, lost for words. Then Angel turns her shocked expression on me. I shrug, letting her know I never heard of Jacques having previous health problems.

"Don't worry about me, ma fleur. I love living, and I ain't going to do nothing else to jeopardize that."

"So what does that mean, exactly?" Heloise says.

We all turn to see her standing under the stone arch. Once she's sure she's attracted our attention, she strolls across the patio like she owns the world, sits in an empty chair, and crosses her legs. By the look of it, she's still waiting for an answer.

Jacques chuckles. "What do you care? I still got you in my will."

Heloise tosses her head back and laughs. I've seen her at a couple of joyous occasions, like Jack and Daisy's baby shower and their third anniversary party, and I've never seen her laugh like that.

Jacques laughs with her. Angel and I raise our eyebrows at each other. I figure we're thinking the same thing—what he said wasn't that funny.

Finally, Heloise simmers down. She leans

forward and stacks her hands on Jacques's knees. "You know I'd rather have you in this world with me than all the money on the planet. You're my everything, Jacques."

Jacques rests his hands over hers. "I ain't going nowhere, baby."

Heloise sits back straight. "You better not. Or I swear I'll kill you while you're in your grave."

I don't know about Angel, but I feel as though I've imposed on their private moment. It's a relief when one of the servers brings us iced tea and croissants and cheese. Angel and I laugh as we listen to Jacques and Heloise's narration of the exciting and crazy years they spent together when they were young and still married.

After they recount their orgies, bar fights, survival of sinking party yachts—first in the middle of the Mediterranean and then in the Indian Ocean—and the story of how they made the best partnership in Hollywood history, they fall quiet.

"Daniel's death," Heloise says, grinning weakly at the terracotta flooring.

"That sobered the hell out of us," Jacques says with a far-off look in his eyes.

Daniel was Daisy's brother, who died when he was hit by a car. Jack mentioned that Daniel and

Daisy were close, and his death messed her up pretty badly.

Heloise shoots to her feet, fast as an arrow. "Since you're good, I better head back to the lions' den."

Jacques moves to stand, but Heloise holds out a hand. "No. Damn, it's time you learn how to rest for real."

Jacques sits back down, and they beam at each other.

"Just say you love me. That's all I need," Heloise says.

"Love you, ma fleur."

I'm shocked to see tears fill Heloise's eyes.

"I love you too." She kisses him on both cheeks and then his lips before saying good-bye to Angel and me.

Heloise crosses paths with Jack and Daisy under the arches. They say good-bye to Daisy's mother and then join us. Since there's only one chair, Daisy sits on Jack's lap as he talks with Jacques about Jack making Mes Fleurs a premium brand. I want to ask Jack how he plans to be a covert operative for some secret organization that Maggie's now part of, a commercial real estate developer, and a winemaker all at the same time. But I pass. I figure it's none of my business what Jack does with his life, and now's not the time to grill him. Jack talks about wine with enthusiasm and, surprisingly, a lot of knowledge about the subject. Fucking Jack… he's a real-life Jack-of-all-trades and my brother. And I need him just like Heloise needs Jacques.

I lean closer to Angel and say in her ear, "Anton invited us to a party tonight. I'm not sure if you—"

"Oh, I know," she says, completely engaged in Jack and Jacques's conversation. I think she likes the idea of her father living out the rest of his days on the vineyard. However, I can't get over the fact that Anton asked her before he asked me. What sort of game is he playing?

"Then we're going?"

"Yeah, we all are," Angel says and then focuses all of her attention on the vineyard talk.

I sit back to stew in my anger. Tonight, I want answers. Anton and I are going to talk man to man.

CHAPTER TWELVE

JAVAR LES

THIRTY-SIX HOURS EARLIER

*J*avar sat on the edge of the bed, waiting. He was positive Mita would be knocking on his door real soon. She'd been wearing tight short shorts and a pink-lace bra. When a woman with her kind of body wanted to get a man ready to fuck, she walked in front of him wearing something like that.

There was a quiet knock on the door. He checked the time again. It was eleven o'clock. Next, Javar checked his phone for any message from Maggie. There was one, which read, *I nailed her. Keep your eyes on her. Call you when I'm on my way to LA.* He'd lain down to rest a little over six hours earlier. Maggie sure did work fast.

Thinking about the way Mita looked in the shorts and bra made his blood flow from his brain to his lower extremity. But then he recalled the last text message from Monroe. She basically had given him permission to do what his job required even if it meant fucking Mita, but he wasn't stupid enough to fall for that. Even a free-spirited woman like Monroe wanted a guy who had a dick only for her. Mita was hot, but she wasn't worth losing the grand prize.

Regardless, Javar quickly took off his pants and shirt, stripping down to his underwear. He made his face look exhausted, and upon opening the door, he flinched as though surprised to see his visitor. "Oh. Hey."

Her gaze ran up and down his physique. "Sorry. Did I wake you?" She grinned.

Javar drew a deep breath in through his nose. "I'm awake now." He flirted with her with his eyes.

Mita's grin grew wider. She quickly looked back over her shoulder. "Do you want company?"

The question was music to Javar's ears. "Do you want to have some fun tonight?"

She watched him with a smoldering gaze. "I want lots of fun."

"Then put on something hot, and I'll meet you in the foyer."

Suddenly her smile faded. "What?"

"I want to show you a good time. Come with me. I promise you won't regret it."

Mita hesitated. For the fourth time, her eyes traveled up and down Javar's body. "Okay. Tonight, you are the maestro."

"Then meet me in the foyer in fifteen?"

"Thirty," she said.

He winked at her. "Your wish is my command."

She seemed to love that saying.

Javar texted Monroe as soon as he closed the door. *Tin Can in MR Hotel. Be there in an hour. Member? Yes? Hope to see you.*

Just in case she wasn't a member, he called Damon and asked that Monroe Blanco be made a special guest for the night. Was he playing with fire? Definitely. Would he get burned? He hoped.

ONE KEY TO SUCCESS IS TO ADMIT THE TRUTH. Javar had to admit that Mita looked smoking hot.

Her plump tits, luscious ass, Jessica Rabbit curves, and cascading dark hair tempted Javar into taking the easy route that night, which would be to go right back to the room and fuck her brains out. She wanted to shag anyway. Once again, if it weren't for Monroe, he would've happily obliged.

"Beautiful automobile. Is it yours?" Mita asked once they were in the driveway.

Javar jumped slightly, distracted by his thoughts. He deactivated the alarm of the midnight-blue Ferrari.

"Um, no, it's a rental."

"Then you live in New York?"

"I have a place there, and in London, Sydney, and Athens." He spoke the truth. He'd learned the best way to make a mark believe he was someone else was to lie as little as possible in the process.

They got into the car, and he put the top down. Mita was asking questions, and he had hoped that the open air would distract her from asking more.

"Fasten your seatbelt," he said before putting the wheels on the road.

They hadn't gotten a mile up Highland before she asked, "Are you married?" as they sat at a red light.

"If I were, I wouldn't be here with you." He looked away from the road to flash her a smile.

She blushed.

The light turned green.

"What about you? Husband? Boyfriend? Lovers?"

"All of the above and none of the above."

"Ha! Was that a riddle?" he asked.

"Isn't life a riddle?"

Her seductive tone made him steal a glance at her. Mita's short dress was up to the top of her thigh. Javar did a double take. Her creamy thighs and the crotch of her lace panties were in plain sight.

Javar found the fact that she was so easy to figure out ironic. "Not so much," he said with a snicker.

Mita spread her legs wider. "Do you want to touch?"

"I would, but I don't want to crash and burn the car."

She rubbed his arm. "You are strong."

Soon the distractions of L.A.'s walking beautiful and heavy traffic garnered Mita's attention. The nightclub was only four blocks away, but every streetlight seemed to stop them.

Javar wasn't prepared when she rubbed his cock. He jumped and then promptly removed her hand. "Listen, love. I'll take care of you soon. No need to rush the night."

She had succeeded in making him anxious. His eyes could barely focus on the loads of tourist stomping the sidewalks.

"The light is green," Mita said, seeming happy to have gotten him worked up.

Javar snapped his face forward. Horns honked behind him. He took off just before it turned red again and was able to make the next three traffic lights without stopping. He took a right off Hollywood Boulevard onto Rockwell and used a card to open the gate of a private subterranean parking lot.

"Is this Monte Red Hotel?" she asked.

"Ah, yes it is," he said, pulling into a reserved space.

Her eyes expanded. "You have membership?"

He smirked cockily. "I'm VIP."

Before he could take his hands off the steering wheel, Mita's lips crashed against his. Her mouth tasted like mint and medicine. Could she have taken pills before leaving?

Javar peeled her off of himself. The time was getting away from them. Tin Can stayed open until six in the morning, but after two o'clock, patrons had to be members of the hotel club to remain, and alcohol was no longer sold but served for free. Basically, no cash was exchanged after that point— bartenders weren't even allowed to receive tips.

"Let's get going, love." He hopped out of the car and searched the garage for Monroe's black Mercedes G-Wagen. There was no sign of it. Javar walked around his car, put an arm around Mita's waist, and lowered the top. They walked to the elevator. She went in for another kiss as soon as they were in. He smooched her until they reached the hotel lobby, grabbing her ass and smashing his hard-on against her. Mita needed to know she was making an impact. The door opened, and their lips parted. To Javar, it was a sobering wake-up call. They had no real chemistry.

They made it to the nightclub, and Mike, a six-foot-five bouncer with the muscle mass of a professional wrestler, opened his arms when he saw Javar.

"Hey..." Mike sang as he gave him a manly kind of hug.

"Bronson," Javar whispered in his ear.

"Bronson, dude, what's been going on?"

"Back in town..." Javar nodded toward Mita. "Lovely lady."

Mike glanced at Mita as if she were just another pretty face—in LA, she was.

"Well, have a good time. I'm here if you need me."

The two seats that Damon had promised to reserve for him at the bar were waiting. They sat. Javar raised his eyebrows at Tiffany, the blond bartender who looked like a young Pamela Anderson. He requested Tiffany's service because she was just what he needed to keep Mita insecure and performing for his attention.

"What can I get for you?" Tiffany asked, flashing her dazzling smile.

Just as he suspected, Mita turned away from the exquisite blonde by setting her elbow on the counter and resting her head in her hand.

"What would you like, love?" he asked Mita.

"That is very English of you."

He frowned. "What's English of me?" he said in his best American accent.

"Love this, love that."

Shit, he thought.

"But I will have red wine," she said.

Javar had two problems. Mita wasn't a drinker, and she'd noticed his colloquial blunder.

"How about sweet vermouth with a touch of

fresh lime juice and vodka?" Tiffany suggested while smiling at Mita.

Javar kept his eyes fixed on Tiffany to force Mita to interact with her. Tiffany knew the drill. He needed to get his date tipsy.

"Do you not have red wine?" Mita asked snobbishly.

Tiffany maintained her friendly disposition. "Not as good as I'm sure you like it. But my signature cocktail is divine. If you don't think so, then I'll dump it down the drain and find the best bottle in the house."

"Why don't you just find it now?"

Tiffany pointed at Javar. "Because this guy wants a gin and tonic, and from what I remember, he doesn't like to drink alone. It may take us a while to find that bottle." Tiffany winked at Mita. "And if I were him, I wouldn't want to start without *you*."

Mita studied Tiffany incredulously. "I will try. Do not make it strong, *per favore*."

Tiffany winked. "*Allora*. Gin and tonic and my house special coming up."

Mita blushed. Javar and Tiffany connected eyes for a second. It was his way of saying, *Thank you* and her way of saying, *You're welcome*.

"So," Javar said, "how did you become a cellist?"

Mita frowned as she watched Tiffany make the drinks. Javar realized she was probably still experiencing the shock of another super-sexy woman so close to them and hoping Tiffany was into her and not him.

Mita shook her head. "I apologize. What did you say?"

Javar sat back in his seat and let himself be loose. "How did you become a cellist? You must be damn good if you're playing for Jacques Blanchard."

She rolled her eyes. "My mother is Chinese and Italian."

Javar studied her, confused. "I'm sorry. Is there a connection between you being Chinese-Italian and a cellist?"

"Yes. To my mother, I was not worth my salt unless I perfected an instrument. I chose the cello."

"Oh… I see. Where did you learn to play so well?"

She sighed hard. "I do not want to talk about my music."

"Okay, then." Javar scratched his ear. "What else interests you?"

She shrugged. "What else is there?"

"Life."

She shrugged indifferently. "I'm alive."

"Right. So why does a beautiful woman such as yourself not have a husband or boyfriend?"

"Because men are pigs—that is why."

"But I'm a man. Am I a pig?"

"Are you?" She watched him curiously. Javar was playing a role, but her question was pretty apt. Was he a pig? And if he was, what did that make her? She had spent most of the night offering him her pussy on a platter.

Tiffany set their drinks in front of them, and Javar was happy for the distraction.

"I made it good for you," Tiffany said to Mita.

Mita smiled timidly. "*Grazie.*"

Tiffany winked at her and then at Javar. Making it good for Mita was code that it was strong enough to have a serious effect on her.

Javar raised his cocktail. "To new friends."

Mita clicked her glass against his, and they both took a drink.

"How do you like it?" he asked.

Mita took another sip. "It is very good."

He grinned. "Tiffany's one of the best."

Mita tilted her head. "Is she a…?"

"A lesbian?" he asked.

"Yes. Is she?"

"You would have to ask her."

Javar knew the answer. He'd fucked Tiffany twice before. She was a beautiful bartender in a city filled with good-looking women. She worked for tips, so she instinctively learned the psychology of beautiful women, and that meant disarming them by any means necessary, even flirting.

After a few seconds of studying Tiffany, Mita flipped her hair and drank some more of the special cocktail. "What about yourself, Bronson? You have no wife?"

"Never wanted one."

She narrowed an eye. "Why not? Do you not like love?"

"I *love* love—especially making it."

Suddenly, she put her hand on his cock and rubbed. "Me too."

Javar didn't flinch, although he wanted to search the room to see if Monroe was watching.

Mita leaned forward. He could feel her breath on his ear. "You are very virile. I want you."

Javar didn't know when he'd decided to not fuck her, but he was sure of that decision.

He raised his hand, and Tiffany came straight

to him. She leaned against the edge of the bar as though doing a pushup. "What can I get you?"

"Get her another," he said.

"Coming up," she said before Mita could object.

Mita took a deep breath as she closed her eyes and ran a hand through her hair. Javar could tell that her head was spinning. One more drink, and she would be down for the count.

The place was filling up fast. There was a stage in front of the club, and go-go dancers took the stage, wiggling their asses. The female dancers humped the stage, and the males banged their cocks against the air. The performance was typical enough to ignore.

"LA is so tasteless," Mita said, grimacing. She was halfway through her second drink. "I don't know why I agreed to this," she shouted over the music.

"What is your favorite city?" he said loudly.

"Where I live now."

"Where is that?"

"Paris."

"You are in LA only to work for Jacques?"

She finished her drink and slammed the glass on the bar top. "Yes, and he didn't call in because he had a heart attack or something." She rolled her eyes and shook her head. "He and I were once lovers."

Javar sat up straight. That was news to him. "Jacques Blanchard?"

"That is what I said. I think he would have married me if it wasn't for his spoiled daughter."

He had to pretend he'd never heard of Angelina Beauchamp. "Why is that?"

She frowned as if she didn't understand his question.

"How did Jacques Blanchard's daughter get in the way of you marrying him?"

"She is jealous, and she said to her father that I am not appropriate for him."

"And you think he listened to her?"

"Of course," she snapped. "She is his daughter!"

Javar knew men like Jacques Blanchard, and they sure as hell didn't let their children run their lives. He knew women like Mita too. Blaming the fact that Jacques didn't choose her on Angelina Beauchamp was the easy way out. So far, he ascertained that all Mita had to offer a man were her pussy, her beauty, and the ability to make beautiful music. A man needed more than that. He needed an interesting woman who could think outside the box—if not all the time then some of the time. A man needed a woman who was passionate about some aspect of the world. A healthy dose of intellectual curiosity didn't hurt either. Javar himself particularly wanted a woman whose pussy and brain were on equal footing. That was why he was so drawn to Monroe.

Suddenly, Mita closed her eyes as though she had fallen asleep without realizing it. Javar placed his mouth to her ear.

"Mita," he whispered.

Her eyes popped open. "Oh, my head." She rubbed her temples.

It wasn't after two in the morning, so he called Tiffany over, tipped her big, and took Mita up to the suite he had paid for. As soon as they were up on the twelfth floor, he took her to the bedroom. Mita fought to keep her eyes open, but she kept losing the battle. She mumbled something about wanting him as she flopped down on the edge of the bed, curled up in a ball, and closed her eyes.

"I'll be back," Javar said.

She didn't respond.

He tiptoed out of the room in time to hear a low knock on the door. He hadn't ordered room service. But he went to the door and looked through the peephole. There stood Monroe Blanco.

Javar checked carefully over his shoulder. Mita hadn't made a peep. He quietly opened the door.

"I saw what you did," Monroe said before he could speak.

He couldn't stop grinning. "What did I do?"

"She squeezed your cock, and you got her too drunk to fuck."

Javar couldn't take his eyes off Monroe's face. She was truly a beauty. Most women would kill for her almond eyes, high cheekbones, and pouty mouth. And her eyes were ice blue. She wasn't thin, though. He had dated many models, and their twiggy bodies never turned him on. Basically, a body like Mita's came along every once in a while. He was sure that was what had enticed Charlie Lord to take a dip. Javar found himself fantasizing about how Monroe's exotic face would look when she climaxed.

"Hello?" Monroe said.

He shook his head and returned to the surface. "If you're not shagging me, then I'm not shagging tonight."

"You mean this morning." Her face lit up when she smiled that way.

"This morning?" Then he realized what she meant. It was after midnight. "Yes. Right... right."

"But..." Monroe slid her index finger down his top and bottom lips. "I'll see you one day soon, and maybe I'll let you shag me." She gently kissed his parted lips.

It happened so fast that Javar didn't get a chance to kiss back. His boner was about to rip the seams of the crotch of his pants. Monroe turned to leave.

"Wait," he whispered as loudly as he could.

Monroe turned to face him but continued to walk backward. "Soon, Mr. Les, very soon."

She spun around and continued to walk away. His eyes veered down to her round ass. She wasn't as stacked as Mita, but she did have a nice ass that he wanted to lick.

"Blimey," he whispered and closed the door.

When he went back into the room, Mita was snoring. He took off her shoes and put the blanket over her. Javar went back into the living room to check for messages from Maggie. He had one. *Arrive in LA in the morning. Where is she?*

He sighed in relief. The assignment was short and almost complete. *Monte Red Hotel.*

Right before he put his phone back in his pants pocket, it dinged.

Be there at 8:00 a.m. Don't let her out of your sight, she wrote.

He sighed impatiently. She'd already told him that. *Aye, aye,* he responded.

Javar put his phone back in his pocket, went back into the bedroom, and lowered the blackout shades. He didn't want the light of day to wake Mita. Thank goodness she was out, because he was exhausted. Tiffany must've made his drink really "good" as well. A combination of the gin and tonic and lack of real sleep made his head light. He crawled into bed next to Mita, and not too long after, he was calling the cows.

Javar dreamt of nothing, but he heard something that sounded like a loud crack and woke up. He quickly felt alone and looked at the other side of the bed. The atmosphere was still dark, but the door was open, so he could see that Mita was not there.

"What the…?" He jumped out of bed and ran into the living room.

"Shit," he said under his breath when he saw his cell phone broken in pieces in front of the door. She must've got into his pockets while he was asleep.

Javar looked for the keys to the car, but they were gone too. Holy fuck, she had taken his fucking car too! He rushed over to the room phone and called Maggie, thankful she'd made him commit her number to memory. "People rely too heavily on their contact list," she'd said. "You lose your phone, and you lose precious time in recovering numbers. Remember the important ones."

Maggie picked up on the second ring. "Yeah, Javar, we're almost there."

"She found my phone, smashed it, and ran off with my car," he said in a rush.

"Fuck," Maggie said emphatically. "To the studio," she told someone else, perhaps the driver. "Where was your phone?"

He sighed hard, realizing he was about to admit to making a big mistake. "In my pocket."

"Fuck."

"I know. I fucked this up really bad."

Maggie sighed regretfully. "Well, are you okay? Do you need me to send a car to pick you up?"

Javar flopped down in a chair and rubbed his temples. "I'll be fine."

"Okay, see you soon. And nice work, Jav. You only lost her in the end. She's a slippery fish."

He wanted to tell her the truth. Sure, he lost in the end, but he was too good at what he did to lose at all. Monroe had stopped by the room last night, and he'd lost focus. But Maggie had never been big on lingering on what went wrong, and he liked that about her.

He thanked her, and they ended the call and his assignment. At least he was free to pursue Monroe Blanco. As a matter of fact, he knew her number by heart as well.

CHAPTER THIRTEEN

I pinch the bridge of my nose. "God damn it." I wanted a nice clean end to this situation. The plan was to go to the hotel, have Vince wait in the car while I talked to our little extortionist, and then let our driver whisk us off to the airport. I'd fly back to Paris and Vince to New York.

I spent most of the flight over the Atlantic discussing a plan with Sir Walter Barnaby and Ariel Hampton about their secret son, who they so recklessly put in the hands of a sociopath. Of course, Ariel was worried about her reputation and her six years of marriage to Clay Davenport, who happens to be an English duke, which makes her a duchess. There's one thing I sussed for sure—Ariel isn't willing to relinquish that title for anything, not even for love. And I can tell she's actually in love with Sir Walter Barnaby. Were he higher in the royal and noble ranks, they would be living happily ever after in snobbery. Regardless, we came to a conclusion, and now I have to fly back to Paris to speak to one pissed-off woman—Laura McIntyre.

I have Grey monitoring Mita's cell phone. She's already tried to call Sir Walter Barnaby, but he knows to not answer. Then she called Laura McIntyre. Mita couldn't reach her and is climbing the walls. She doesn't know that Laura has been detained by local authorities for attempting to sneak Abel out of the country in a private airplane.

They'll be holding her until I arrive. However, I had Lila Brown, an agent out of London, explain the child's true parentage to Laura, who didn't take it so well. So now I have to lay out very clearly what her options are and how her decisions can hurt the one person she's been trying to protect.

But damn, Javar is not making this easy—I hoped to take care of business and get the hell out of town. It's not like him to make such a mistake. He left his cell phone in his pocket? When we worked together on our first assignment, he almost learned that lesson the hard way—he happened to wake up in the middle of the night and find Yvette Maynard, the woman who was out to get Jack, digging through his pants pockets. But he had been smart enough to keep his phone in a drawer. The lesson was that crafty people never trust anyone because they themselves can't be trusted. Therefore, always assume that the mark will go through your pockets while you are asleep.

"Are you sure Mita Capelli is going back to the studio?" Vince asks.

I blink, making myself present again. "Positive. She has to get her things before boarding her flight, which takes off in two hours."

Vince sighs and rests his head on the seat. "I don't know about this, Mags."

We had a long talk on the way back to LA. He's still afraid that what I do is too dangerous. I was serious when I asked if he wanted to be equal partners in my business. He told me he preferred to stay in his current career.

Vince is a media mogul, and I know he loves what he does. I have a feeling that I might have insulted him when I asked him to get on board with my new and exciting life adventure.

I gaze out the window. We're speeding down a residential street of Spanish-style homes. The morning traffic is horrendous, but Ben is a professional driver who knows all the back roads.

"Sorry if I offended you by asking you to give up your world and join mine," I say. "It's just that I don't want my job to jeopardize our marriage."

I turn my worried gaze on Vince and see that he's already studying me.

"I like you working with Sir Walter Barnaby on trying to schmooze his ordeal with the public more than your sneaking into apartments in search of evidence and then confronting rich, morally questionable men with whatever you find. I mean, this guy gave his child away to a woman who used the kid to extort men."

I rub Vince's thigh. "I know, babe. That's pretty terrible."

"And those goons that came out after he asked if anyone else knew his secret—what if I wasn't there?"

"Lian would've gone inside with me. I promise. And he's definitely capable of handling those goons."

Vince purses his lips. "Listen, babe, do you really want to do this?"

I nod enthusiastically. "I really do. It's not Sir Walter Barnaby or Mita or even David McIntyre I want to do this for. It's Abel. Can you imagine growing up in the same shitty situation he's in? I want to make sure he's with the right people—that's all."

Vince reaches over to massage the back of my neck. I close my eyes and indulge in the way it feels.

"Then I'm with you," he says.

I sigh with relief and open my eyes. "Thanks, babe. And I guess it felt so right to have you on this case with me that I got carried away."

"No way. I liked being on this with you. I had fun." He shrugs. "And maybe we can work something out."

My heart lights up, and I smile. I can hardly believe I heard him say that. "What do you mean?"

Now he's smiling too. "I work with you sometimes. And sometimes you work with me. How about that for splitting the difference?"

I grunt, intrigued. It wouldn't be so bad helping A&Rt Media on a project every now and then. With Mo&Ma, I used my powers of persuasion to help spoiled, entitled, and manipulative public figures with PR. Vince would never require me to step over to the dark side, and neither would Jack. And of course, I'll never choose personal jobs that cross that moral line. I'm not flying back to Paris and then to Switzerland to help Sir Walter Barnaby and his lover, who are both married to other people. Like I told Vince, I have Abel's best interest at heart.

I hold out my hand for Vince to shake. "All right, then. When you need me, you have me, and when I need you, I have you."

He shakes. "Deal."

He guides my face closer to his, and we kiss with our lips and tongues until the car stops next to a palm tree in front of Jacques's studio in Hancock Park.

I look out the window. "We arrived just in time."

Come hell or high water, I would've had a talk with Mita before she boarded that flight back to Paris. Thank goodness she's storming out of the house right now with her suitcase and weekend bag.

I pat Vince's thigh. "I'll be back, babe."

"Be careful," he says.

I wink at him and shut the door behind me.

Mita sees me and stops before she reaches Javar's blue Ferrari. I've never laid eyes on her in my life, but perhaps her instincts are telling her that I'm the trouble she's wanted to avoid all morning.

"Mita Capelli," I say when I'm closer.

She squints at me harshly although she doesn't take another step. "Who are you?"

I wrinkle my nose while mentally going through the many ways this could go. I force myself to remember that I have to step away from the situation emotionally. Yeah, I'm angry that she had the balls to try to ruin Charlie's relationship. I'm disgusted by the fact that she's screwed with people's lives, including that of an innocent child. I want to grab her by the shoulders, shake her, and yell, "Don't you even care about what you're doing to that poor kid?" But I get a grip and get to work.

"I'm your worst nightmare, Mita Capelli," I say.

She folds her arms. "And how is that?"

I hold out my hands. "First of all, you're going to give me the keys to Bronson's car, or I'll take them from you."

"That is not his name—it's Javar Les."

I clench my lips, conveying with my expression that not only do I mean business, but I'm not shedding any light on the subject of Javar-Bronson's identity.

Mita looks down at the keys in her hands. "And you're Maggie."

I nod. "I'm Maggie."

"You have been very busy girl, Maggie."

"And so have you. So keys, now."

She hesitates then sets the keys in the palm of my hand.

"So let's just get to it. Abel Barnaby?"

Her mouth falls open. Great—she's lost for words.

"Tests conclude that he's no relation to you or Ralph McIntyre, whom you've extorted into paying twenty thousand dollars a month. And he's definitely no relation to my cousin, Charlie Lord."

She shrugs a shoulder defiantly. "So what? Charlie still fucked me, and Angelina will know."

I scratch my eyebrow. What a feisty, crazy bitch. I figure that in true sociopath form, her emotions are clicking right now.

I chuckle bitterly. "You see, you still think you can win this. I'm going to give you a moment to absorb something. One call to my cousin's fiancée, one conversation, and you're ass *will* go to jail for extortion. And I hope very much you test me."

We glare into each other's eyes. I'm not even close to flinching. She cuts eye contact first, and when she looks at me again, she's blinking rapidly.

She shrugs defiantly. "They are all bad people. I—"

"You paid a woman named Annabelle Kumar

to take the child whenever he wasn't with Laura McIntyre. From all I've learned, the child doesn't even know you as the parent. You've used this poor kid as a pawn in your scam. I should send your ass to jail for the sake of justice."

I wait for her response. Her lips are pursed tightly, and her chin quivers slightly. It doesn't surprise me that she's the type to regress to crying when her house of cards is blown down.

She slaps herself on the chest. "I am the person who made sure the child was safe. They were going to take him to an orphanage."

"But instead, you decided he could be more effective serving your purpose."

Tears fill her eyes, and she wipes away the ones that fall. "I…"

I take a deep breath and hold it in before releasing it with force. "Actually, Abel is lucky you tried to extort my flesh and blood. He's only two, and I'm going to see to it that the rest of his life is filled with normalcy."

Suddenly, Mita's lips form in to a sinister smirk. "Who with? Laura? Walter? Oh, with Ariel? You think I'm the witch, but they are the devil." She doesn't drop that evil smirk.

Now I really get close to her face. "I doubt that.

But I'll tell you this, and mark my words—if I ever get wind of you extorting another human, I'm going to take you all the way down. If you ever want to try me, then please do. I want you to cross me, because you disgust me, and I would rather have you in jail than on the streets."

Her eyes narrow to slits. "Are you finished?"

"Do we have an understanding?"

It takes a moment, but finally, she says through clenched lips, "We do."

I step back. "Good."

A cab pulls up in front of the house, and Javar gets out. Mita turns her back on us and stomps off and into the house.

"Magnolia," he says rushing to me with open arms.

I toss him the keys before he reaches me.

"How did it go?" he asks.

"The way I thought." I sigh and then smile. It's time to change the mood. "You, my friend, look a mess but still gorgeous as hell."

Finally, we hug.

"You smell like airplane." He points his chin toward the road. "Here comes company. Who's the bloke?"

I turn and see Vince walking toward us. Jeez, I

think Javar threatens him. They've never met before, and it's high time they do.

"My husband, Vince."

"You married him?"

"I sent you two invitations, and you never responded."

"To what address?"

"Your London address."

"I hadn't been there in ages. You should've called."

"I did."

"Oh, right," he says quickly. "I abhor weddings."

I roll my eyes.

"You must be Javar Les," Vince says with a hand outstretched.

"Why, yes, and you're the lucky man."

They shake hands, and then Vince wraps his arm around my waist. "That's how I see it," he says.

"Right… right…" Javar says in a distracted way. "Your friend Monroe—"

I slap my forehead. It took one word to understand why he made the mistake of leaving his phone in his pocket. "Monroe. That's why you slipped? What's going on between you two?"

"Nothing," he says in a high-pitched voice.

"Shit. It was my fault. I wanted her to come and make Mita feel insecure, but I forgot you have a thing for her."

He shakes his head. "No, I don't."

I cock my head and narrow an eye.

"Well, just a hint of a thing."

I glance up at Vince to make sure he's following this.

"Javar, I like you, and when I like someone, I try to give them good advice. So here it goes: now is not the time to pursue Monroe. She's still confused and finding herself. The last time she screwed around with…"

"Go on, say it," Javar says.

I glance at Vince, and he shrugs. He knows me well enough to be aware that I'm going to be brutally honest from this point on.

"Well, the last time she screwed around with an egomaniac in transition, it was Charlie, and we all know how that ended for both of them."

"So… you think I'm an egomaniac."

I shrug and twist my mouth sheepishly. "At least you're in transition."

Javar looks back and forth between Vince and me before landing on me. "Never mind. Monroe and I—she's on a flight to Montreal. She left this morning."

I flinch, taken aback. "Really?" I'm surprised she didn't call and tell me she was going to Montreal. She tells me everything.

"She said she's acting in a movie that Ship Gorman's directing. He lost his lead actress at the last minute, so he asked her to fill in."

"Wow," I say.

"Yeah, wow," Vince says.

There's a honk, and we all turn to see a white taxicab in front of the house. Mita appears on the doorstep.

"You are a liar!" she yells at Javar as she zooms past us.

"I would say she's pissed," Javar says.

"I would say so," I confirm.

The driver hops out of the car to help with her bags, but she waves him back inside, rushes her luggage into the backseat with her, and slams the door. The taxi speeds off. She must've told him to get the hell out of here as fast as he can.

"Good," I say, grimacing as the tail end of the car disappears. "My job is done here." But at the same time, it's only just begun.

CHAPTER FOURTEEN

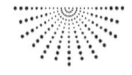

CHARLIE LORD

"*I*t's in a neighboring vineyard," Angelina says from the bathroom.

I've already asked her twice where the party is happening. Daisy and Jack have juiced up their airplane and are now on their way back to the US. Daisy felt some cramps earlier. Since she's at the end of her third trimester and has already lost one child, they decided to leave so they can be near her team of doctors in San Francisco.

Personally, I'm not in the party mood. I'm jet lagged, and it didn't help that all through last night, Angel and I couldn't stop touching, caressing, and making love. The day has been so full of the right things—laughs, family, food, and me playing one of

Jacques's guitars for him—that we don't need to jam another activity into it.

I yawn. "Aren't you tired? I am."

"Yes, but Anton really wants us to go."

"He'd be tired too if he'd cared to join the rest of us today." I plop down on the foot of the bed to put on one of my shoes.

"He's one of the hosts of the party, so he had to help set up. Listen, I'm tired too, Charlie, but I hardly ever see Anton, and he really wants us to go…" She walks out of the bathroom, wearing a slinky red cocktail dress that makes her cinnamon skin look radiant. "We don't have to stay long. Let's dance a few times, have a glass of Chateaux Trois Fils, and walk back."

Angel sits beside me and puts on a shoe. I'm still blown away by how drop-dead gorgeous she looks in that dress. When I first met her, she had long hair that she kept tied up. Her mane has grown all the way back. She's such an exquisitely beautiful woman, whether her hair is pinned up or hanging down. Tonight, I like the way the strands spray over the flawless skin of her shoulders and the wings of her back.

I run my palm up her tight dancer's thighs.

"Wow. Are you really asking me to go out after you put that on?" Not to mention how good she smells.

She squeezes my wrist to stop my hand from completing the journey. "We're already late."

I protest with a sigh. Angel pats me on the thigh and slips on her other shoe. There's no way I can convince her to stay in tonight, so we put the finishing touches on ourselves before walking out into the night. The air is warmish but only because of the humidity as Angel and I take the dirt road away from the vineyard. I gaze up. The moon's a waning crescent that's being chased by sprays of clouds.

"It's nice out, isn't it?" Angel asks.

"It is…"

Our satisfying day has merged into this magnificent sort of night. I don't deserve to exist in this moment. Each second that goes by without me telling Angel the truth about what happened with Mita makes me feel more like a fraud.

"So about the wedding. Any ideas?" Angel asks.

I pull my attention away from my thoughts and gaze at her beautiful face. The slight but luminous moon and the lanterns that line the dirt road are our only light. Deep down, I'm asking myself if there's going to be a wedding. I want to tell her the truth—I really do.

Angel snaps her fingers. "Earth to Charlie."

I shake my head. "Sorry, babe. I am tired."

She hugs my arm and snuggles up against me. "I know. You can go back to the cottage and rest."

"No way. I'm going with you."

She cocks her head to the side and studies me with one eye closed. "You do trust me, don't you?"

"Of course. It's the other guys I don't trust."

"Are you referring to Anton?" She's grinning.

"Maybe. There's something about him."

After watching me for a few moments, she grunts inquisitively.

"What is it?" I ask as we make a turn and walk up the main road.

"It's not only you. It's him too."

I feel my forehead crash into a frown. "What have I ever done to him besides be engaged to you?"

She sighs. "Can we stop beating that drum? He's not in love with me. He just thinks..." Angel drops her gaze to the ground.

"He thinks what?" I snap.

"I don't want you two to fight. We're practically

family, for goodness' sake. Anton just has to get to know you."

I stop walking. "I want to know what he said about me."

Angel groans and jerks her head from side to side. "Come on, Charlie. Let it go."

"Why? What's done is done. He doesn't like me, and hell, I don't like him either, but I haven't said shit to you about it. He's fighting fucking dirty."

Angel wraps her arms around me, but I'm not ready to hug her back.

"Anton can say what he wants. It doesn't change the fact that I'll always love you. But he's just being protective. No one's ever good enough for me in his eyes." She takes me by the shoulders. "But you are, Charlie. And he'll see that over time."

I want to explode. Who gives a fuck what Anton sees over time? I don't! But instead of shouting, I take a deep breath to calm myself. The guy is important to Angel, and I love her. I repeat that to myself two more times before lowering my face toward her pleading gaze and kissing her on the lips. My head spins. Two and a half years after we first got together, and I'm still surprised by that intoxicated feeling I have when I kiss her.

Talk about the wedding continues as we walk

on. Angel throws out some ideas for locations—
Paris, here at the vineyard, New Iberia.

"Whatever you want," I say.

"All the energy it takes to pull off one day—
invitations, venues, wedding cake, flowers, la-di-da,
di-da, di-da…" She sighs as if the thought over-
whelms her.

"It's a lot to do."

"And the pressure to do it," she says.

"I'm not pressuring you."

"No, but *they* are."

"Who are *they*?"

"Daisy, Papa, our friends, society! If we don't do
the full ceremony thing, we'll so hear about it."

I grunt curiously. I've never taken Angel for
someone who cares what others think, even those
closest to us.

The only sound left is our feet beating the road
and the faint contemporary disco beats in the air.

"This way," Angel says.

We take a right and head down a steep hill. A
modest-sized white stone chateau with tall trees
attached to one end is in full view. The music is
louder. Disco lights are flashing from behind the
estate.

"Anyway, tonight isn't about the drudgery of

planning a wedding. It's about fun!" Angel dances through a redbrick trail that runs between two fields of grapevines. The closer we get, the more I'm filled with dread. At least she's smiling and happy. Usually I'm infected by her glee, but not tonight.

There are groups of people ahead of us and more behind us. I sigh. We're not alone anymore, which means now it's time to do a better job of pretending I want to be here.

We walk out of the grapevines, and the grounds are more illuminated. There are a lot of people here too—they're sitting on the lawn or moving in the same direction we're going. Someone calls Angel's name, and she jumps to face the direction the voice has come from. After taking a moment to search past faces, she jumps again, screams, and bolts toward three women.

I stand here with this silly smile plastered on my face until she drags her friends back toward me. They're speaking in French so fast that I can hardly keep up.

"*Je vous…*" Angel starts.

"I know who this is—Charles Lord," says the one with the long, shaggy black hair and bangs.

I'm trying to place her face, but I can't. Angel

has a strange smile on her face, and I really hate that this awkward moment put it there.

Angel continues introducing the three women. I'm hardly focused on them but do manage to learn that their names are Roxanne, Jeanne-Marie, and Sophia, but I'm still too distracted to distinguish one from the other.

"You don't remember me, no?" the one with bangs says.

"Apparently not," Angel says, still wearing the fake smile.

I know she's uncomfortable. We've run into more than a few women who knew me when I was —as Maggie's group of friends used to put it—a scoundrel. At first, it pissed Angel off and made her question why she decided to involve herself with me in the first place. Convincing her that I wasn't the same person became easier with each encounter. The last two incidences, once when we were in the Apple Bar on Sixth Avenue and once while lying on Paradise Beach in Mykonos, Angel basically stood beside me, engaged in the conversation, until I dismissed the women. Hell, I probably did fuck them all at some point, but more than likely, I was drunk or didn't care enough to remember them. It took long conversations filled with introspection to get Angel to believe that I was a changed man and didn't need to fuck to forget my misery anymore. However, tonight I feel as if we've reverted to the early days when I didn't have her complete trust.

I put my arm around Angel's waist, and she remains stiff. "Sorry. I don't remember you."

The woman bats her eyelashes at me as if her flirtatious expression is supposed to jog a memory.

Angel shakes her head. "Anyway, we danced together at Moulin Rouge in Paris for a season."

The blonde with the short hair and lots of black shit around her eyes changes the subject by saying that she heard she was one of the lead dancers in *The Dazzler*.

"Yes, I was, but my father fell ill, so…" Angel's just humoring them now.

Finally, a familiar voice calls, "Angelina Beauchamp!"

Angel's face lights as if the king of the vineyard is summoning her. She says good-bye to the women and traipses off, leaving me alone with them. *Why the hell did she do that?*

"So, Charles Lord, you don't remember fucking me," the one with shaggy bangs says.

The other two women look amused by her question.

My first instinct is to ignore her and catch up with Angel. However, I'm pissed as fuck. "Don't you see me with my fucking fiancée?"

She blinks as if she's stunned and stung. "I asked an easy question."

I'm shaking my head emphatically. "No, I fucking don't remember you. I wouldn't remember you." I take a deep breath and try to get a grip. What the fuck am I saying? I glance back over my right shoulder and then over my left to see if Angel is anywhere around. I can't see her. "Listen, I don't remember."

"You have already said this," the one with the messy ponytail says. I think I offended them all by being so aggressive.

"Right. And I'm sorry about that. I was different then. I love Angel."

"Ah… I see. The girl with the golden twat," Ponytail says.

They giggle.

I glare at all three of them. Why did I expect them to have an ounce of gentleness? I mean, sure, I mouthed off, but who brings up a one-night stand —and probably not even that—when a guy's with his woman? A troublemaker, that's who. I trot away from them without saying good-bye or anything.

There are so many fucking people here. Where the fuck did they all come from? So far, I don't recognize a soul. I've met a lot of Angel's French friends, and I have my own friends in this country too. Every now and then, someone from my circle will know someone from hers. Then there are people I've worked with and those who recognize me from playing on stage with Jacques. Right now, I need a familiar face to take the edge off. Angel is pissed at me—this I know for sure.

I continue to follow the music and search the faces of everyone I pass, near and far. Fucking Anton got exactly what he wanted. I'm positive he planned to steal Angel away from me and make me feel it. I'm stomping across the grass. Part of me wants to give up and go back to the cottage and sulk until Angel returns tonight.

I walk under a canvas, weaving past partygoers. The music is good, so most people dance where they stand, bopping their heads and singing along while drinking wine. I know to look where most of the dancing is taking place. That's where I'll usually find Angel. My heart beats rapidly as I move closer to the stage, dreading the big what-ifs—what if she's off canoodling with Anton? What if she knows the truth about Mita and me? But there is no *Mita and me.* What if she's been in love with Anton the whole time we've been together? Now my heart is beating even faster. Its palpitations slow immediately when I catch her in front of the stage twirling, kicking, twisting her hips, and dancing like her life depends on it. She's smiling, and Anton isn't her dance partner.

An arm is against my arm. I turn my head. Anton is next to me.

"I want to talk. Follow me." He walks off before I can respond.

My heart speeds up again, not from fear but from anger. I have a mind to stay put and basically tell him to go fuck himself. But he's right—we do have some talking to do. Anton's only about an inch or so shorter than I am, so I easily catch sight of him. He's walking on the outskirts of the dance floor and the canopies for food and drinks. He moves up a path through the trees. I catch up to him once we make it to the side entrance of the manor. I'm still fuming but, at the same time, feel funny, as though I'm being called to the principal's office.

"What's this about?" I ask as we walk down a wide hallway with green marble tile.

"One moment," he says.

I feel my frown deepening. The only thing that's keeping me from stopping and insisting he tell me now or I go back to the party is the group of portraits on the walls. Men in wigs and buttoned-up shirts and women with pale shoulders and their hair in bangs are watching us. Those paintings can't be original. If they were, they'd be worth a fortune. Anton and I are the only ones in the hallway. Except for our momentary presence, tonight would present a perfect opportunity for an art thief to come in and steal them.

We enter a ballroom that has a lot of antique-looking furniture. Porcelain vases are on shelves. Some of them are filled with fresh roses, which is probably why the room smells so flowery.

Anton sits in one of two chairs, which have crooked wooden legs and pink-and-gold embroidered flower patterns. I sit down in the other seat, sigh, and rest my foot on my leg.

"Now. What the hell is this all about?" I ask.

Anton studies me with one eye narrowed. "This is about a woman, a very sensual woman, sexy—she loves to make a man desire her."

I drop my foot back on the floor as impatience races through me. "What woman? Angel? That sounds nothing like her."

He cracks a tiny smile. "Not in the least."

"Then who the fuck are you talking about?"

"Mita. Mita Capelli. You are familiar with her, no?"

What a way to make me feel as if this big, wide room is closing in on me. My dazed look falls on the heavy drapery. The curtains are pulled over what I assume are floor-to-ceiling windows. I think I need air, and I certainly need to breathe.

I cough into my fist. "What about Mita Capelli?"

"She played me a video. Have you seen it?"

My eyes are blinking slower than normal. What the hell is happening right now? I could continue to lose my composure or handle this like a man.

So I breathe in deeply through my nose and let it out forcefully. "You're talking about the video of Mita and me?"

Anton shrugs and throws his hands up. I guess that's the full extent of his response.

I sigh again and scratch my eyebrow. How in the hell can I approach this? "The video was manipulated."

He laughs bitterly.

"The time aspect of it at least. Yeah, she had me for a moment, but the video didn't show me pushing her off me. It took me all of seventeen seconds to do that. I had Maggie check it out, and she confirmed it."

"Maggie saw the video?"

"Yeah. Listen, Angel and I were new. I just met her, and I had already fucked up, so when I made this second fuckup…" I shake my head. There is no way Angel will forgive me.

"What was your first fuckup?"

His expression demands an answer, and I'm in no position to withhold my response. "I let a woman give me a blow job. I should've stopped her too." I scratch my other eyebrow. What the fuck? Listening to myself, I sound like a dope, a bad boyfriend, a lousy fiancé, a fucking philanderer. I look Anton in the eyes, wondering if he's disgusted by me. "I was different then."

He groans and shifts in his seat before resting his elbows on his thighs to rub his scalp. Then he sits up straight. "I love Angelina." He points at me. "Is not what you think."

I'm trying to get that through my thick head. Perhaps he isn't into her, but if she leaves me, then the door is wide open for him. Would he refuse to walk through it? Hell no. I've seen the way he's looked at her tits.

I shrug indifferently.

"I am not good enough for her," he says.

I scoff and roll my eyes. "And neither am I?" Is that what the fuck he's trying to say?

He purses his lips. "This I do not know. She says you are *magnifique*. Usually, I trust her judgment. But how can I trust what she feels about you when she does not know what you have done?"

I watch him, speechless.

Anton slowly rises to his feet. "I will give you one day to tell her, or I will tell her."

His head is down as he walks out with unsteady steps. I sort of think it was just as difficult for him to have this conversation as it was for me. He's right, though. The only thing standing between me and Angel working on a solid happily ever after is this lie between us.

I stand but feel dizzy, so I sit back down. All I can do at this point is let the chips fall where they may. If Angel decides to leave me forever, at least there will be no secrets between us.

I somehow find my way outside. It dawns on me that we couldn't hear the music from inside the house. Some kid is screaming into the microphone and calling it singing. Even more people have arrived, and there's a lot going on. Truth be told,

I'd rather not look for Angel. She should have a good time without me. I'm not quite in the moment as I walk. One face merges into the next. There's loud chatter, laughing, and singing, but to me, it all sounds muffled. Could this be the last twenty-four hours of my relationship with Angel? I wouldn't even know how to fall in love with another woman.

CHAPTER FIFTEEN

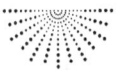

CHARLIE LORD

My steps are heavy. I don't notice the moonlight or the grapevines. The sweet smell of the earth evades my senses. If I were a weeping man, I'd be bawling my eyes out. When I make it back to Jacques's estate, I feel slightly relieved. I make it to the back of the castle and walk in a direction perpendicular to the lit swimming pool. Madeleine is doing the backstroke. I cut my gaze away from her. If only I could be so easygoing. Instead, I have a lot of heaviness on my mind and a bottle of wine waiting by the bed to help me bear the weight of it all.

"You're back early," Jacques says.

I turn around and look up, but I smell the

cigarette smoke before I see Jacques standing on the lower balcony.

"My last one before I quit for good." He shows me the cigarette. "It's down to the butt. But I have one more. You want it?"

I recall the first time Jacques and I smoked together. I hadn't smoked in three years, at least not a cigarette, but I wasn't going to pass on sharing one with Jacques Blanchard. Since then, no cigarette has touched my lips.

"If I can remember how to do it!" I say, suddenly feeling a little better.

Jacques's chuckle is infectious. "Then I'll just keep it to myself, but I want to talk to you for a minute. You got some time?"

"Hell yeah!" I always have time for Jacques. "How do I get up there?"

"I'll come down. Gotta join my woman for a swim anyway."

I keep forgetting Jacques has a new woman in his life. Madeleine has been gone for most of the day. She's a fashion designer and a pretty well-known one at that. She had meetings to attend, but she delegated tasks so that she could spend a lot of time up here with Jacques. That's the thing about

Jacques—beautiful women fall for him, and they fall hard.

Soon he walks out of the door of the atrium with a fresh cigarette.

"This is my last," he says.

I snicker. Angel's always on him about smoking, and now she has an ally in Madeleine.

"You look better. Are you feeling better?" I ask.

"As long as I don't overdo it. Did my Angel outdance you tonight?"

"Yeah. I lost her in the party mix."

Jacques smiles as he looks off toward the pool, seeming amused by his thoughts. Suddenly, he snaps into serious mode. "So I wanted to talk to you about something."

My expression opens to whatever he has to say.

"I want you to partner with me. Well… more than that." He smoothly lights his *last* cigarette, or at least that's what he calls it. "I want you to take over…" He takes a puff. "Take MOS. It's got to be the, you know, biggest stress I clean off my plate."

My mouth opens, but I don't have words for this. I swallow hard and try again. "But you…"

"It ain't like it used to be. Shit is so technical these days. I remember scoring with full orchestras no matter what." Jacques shakes his head. "They want it fast. I walk into the studio, and half my crew is doing this shit." He makes like he's texting. "I have no more patience for it."

The thought of what he's willing to give up stuns me. "You have a pretty successful studio, Jacques. What's it worth? One or two million?"

"I'm not going to sell it to you for that much."

"There's no way I'll pay less than what it's worth. Hell, I owe double the price and more."

Jacques grins smoothly as he blows a cloud of smoke out of his mouth. "Then you'll buy it?"

Shit. I sort of want to sleep on it, but my instincts tell me that it's a no-brainer. Even Jack would say that, and he's the man who always wants to comb through the details before he even considers a deal.

"What about your regulars?"

"Bullshit, they all know you're the man. Hell, you know how to use new computer shit better than I do. I'm just the ears guy. Sit back. Listen. Don't touch. And tell them what I want. You got the hands and the ears." He smashes out his cigarette even though he has half of it left. "There. I quit."

Madeleine calls in French from the pool for Jacques to join her.

He tells her to wait a moment and then sets his smile on me. "She's a beautiful woman, that Madeleine, inside and out. She's got me doing shit I never dreamed of doing. I have to keep reminding her that I'm heading toward sixty."

"That's because you look twenty years younger."

"On the outside, but my heart made me wake the hell up and realize I'm getting older and wearing myself out." He watches Madeleine, beaming. "I ain't been like this since Justine."

"Madame Beauchamp?"

"Every man's got at least one love of his life. He's a hell of a lucky guy when he gets two." He's still smiling at Madeleine.

I'm close to spilling my guts about Mita and how she tried to blackmail me, but instead, I hold out my hand. "I'm in. But under one condition."

He takes my hand. "What's that?"

"You don't sell it to me for a penny less than what it's worth. I'm not trying to catch a deal here, Jacques. Midnight Orleans Studios is *your* legacy. And even after I buy it, you can use it. Hell, you can take a shit in every toilet just to get your kicks when you want, whenever you want."

He laughs and then shakes my hand. "You got it, brother."

We both turn to see Angelina and Anton walking toward us.

"There you are," she says.

Anton starts taking steps backward. "I told you he left. Now…" He thumbs over his shoulder. "I'm going back."

I wait for him to give a look of warning and thereby rub his ultimatum in my face, but he doesn't. I guess he's a stand-up guy after all.

"Why did you leave without telling me?" she whines.

Shit, I wasn't thinking about her making that walk back home alone. "Sorry, babe. I was just…"

Madeleine calls Jacques again. He tells her he's coming and kisses Angelina, and they hug.

"We'll talk more tomorrow," he says.

I nod.

Angel's curious gaze moves from Jacques's face to mine.

Jacques walks away and then turns back to face us. "I would invite you, but this night swim is for the grown and sexy." He laughs.

Angel grimaces, making a squeamish face, and I

chuckle, although it is sort of hard to imagine Jacques having a pool-fucking session with a woman almost half his age.

Now that we're alone, Angel and I stare into each other's eyes. All the love I have for her rushes to the surface.

"I'm sorry," we say at the same time.

We smile.

"Please let me apologize for leaving you with the one-eyed witches. I had no idea they would try to embarrass me and you that way."

"I really didn't remember her. And I have a past, babe. You know that." Knowing myself, I could've been drunk, high, or just serially fucking women without really caring who they were as people.

She sighs. "I know. I guess I was jealous, and that's why I left. I was being immature."

Here's another time tonight where I don't have the words to respond. Perhaps it's because the truth is lodged in my heart and I want to tell Angel about it. I wrap my arms around her, and she reciprocates.

"We better get away from the pool before I'm traumatized for life," she says.

"Hey, do you want to go back to the party? You were dancing up a storm."

She takes me by the hand. "No," she says with sincerity. "I want to return to our bed, make love, sleep, and then make love again."

Is now the time to confess, or do I make love to her one last time? I nod stiffly and let her walk me back to the cottages. My heart feels like a two-ton boulder. I take a deep breath here and there to keep myself from breaking down.

We walk inside the cottage. It's nice and cool. A fresh platter of bread and cheese is on the kitchen table. Ines, the kitchen cook, has someone bring a small serving every night before bed. If we hadn't made it back before eleven, then she would've had the platter brought back and put in the refrigerator.

"Can I just hold you tonight?" I ask Angel.

That's all I want us to do—strip out of our clothes so I can feel her soft, warm body against me.

She pets the side of my face. "Charlie, are you okay?"

I shrug. It's all I can do to keep from crying.

Her eyes narrow with concern. "What's wrong, baby?"

I purse my lips and shake my head. "I just want to hold you. Can I?"

Angel kisses my neck. "Sure. Absolutely."

"Where's the zipper?" I ask.

She reaches for it. "Here on the side."

I take the clasp from her and unzip her dress and then pull it over her head. She's not wearing a bra, but the way her pussy looks in those red lace panties makes me change my mind. I guide her onto the bed and take off her shoes. Next, I kick my shoes off and strip down to nothing. Angel must be able to recognize the look in my eyes. My fucking lust is on fire. I move toward her, take her by the waist, lift her, and move her farther back on the bed. I keep her panties on at first. Her pussy smells like sweat and her natural juices. I love how she jumps when I stab her clit through the thick crotch of her panties with my tongue. I stroke it some more. The hotter, wetter, and louder she gets, the more turned on I become.

"Oh, Charlie…" she whimpers.

I snatch her panties, tug them down her legs and over her feet, and throw them somewhere behind us. I suck and eat and taste. I know she's not feeling much stimulation right now, but this indulgence is for me. First, I want her wetness all over my face. I tongue fuck her. I squeeze her sexy, sexy ass. And now, I'm ready to make her scream. My mouth clamps down on that hard-and-soft spot and works with my tongue to suck and stroke in unison until she screams and moans. I only stop when I can hear she's about to come. Her body goes limp, but I start again, and stop again before she comes. I do that one, two, three, four, five times. She's breathing heavily. I feel the constant shivering in her legs, and the knot of her clit is more responsive. And now I won't stop. I don't stop. Angel is hip to my method. I only binge eat her pussy on special occasions.

"Umm…" I moan and can barely hear myself.

Angel is all kinds of loud. Her fingers are digging into my scalp, and her ass is rubbing the mattress, needing to get reprieve from my consistent and gentle sucking.

Finally, she screams the loudest, and I wait for it. Sprays of her liquid shoot me in the neck and chin as her body jerks. Fuck, I'm so hard that I'm about to explode. I open her legs and crash my dick into her hot wetness.

"Oh fuck." I groan. She's always too fucking tight when I'm overexcited like this.

"Go slow," she whispers. Her warm breath in my ear makes that really hard to do.

I try. My strokes are slow and steady. Damn, this feels so fucking good, and I'm working like an engine chugging up a steep hill in an effort to make it last. But the next thing I know, a force of pleasure crashes into my cock, and it feels too fucking good to not shout as loud as I can.

Damn. It's over. I lick, suck, and chew up her salty neck all the way to her sensual mouth.

"Um…" The way her mouth tastes makes me want to grow another boner.

"Wow, that was amazing," she whispers once our lips part.

"You're amazing."

I roll off of her and draw her against me.

"Gosh, I'm tired, but I don't want to go to bed without showering," she says.

"Can I join you?"

"Charlie, I really want to get in and get out."

"No funny business, I promise. I only want to wash your body." I gently stroke her hip.

Angel sucks air between her teeth. "You musicians are born with the right touch."

I laugh. "So is that a yes?"

She slips out of my arms as she scoots to the edge of the bed. "Come on."

I leap out of bed like a happy puppy and wrap my arms around her as we walk to the glass shower. Since we're in a good moment, I decide we should stay in it. Angel makes the water warm, and I soak a loofah with soap and water and buff the flawless cinnamon skin of her back. I move down to her ass and then hips. My dick grows as I turn her around and face her perfect breasts.

"Arms up," I say thickly.

I fight the impulse to suck on her nipples and instead scrub one armpit and the other. Angel grins, amused, as I wipe her belly. She knows her tits are my addiction. I used to suck on them so much that her nipples would get so sore. We had to slowly wean me off of them, but damn if my cock doesn't get a jolt every time I see them.

Now that all but my favorite parts of her have suds on them, I smirk at her.

Angel chuckles. "Can I put my arms down now?"

I lift a finger. "One sec." I take as much of her right breast as I can into my mouth, sucking and scraping her nipple with my teeth. When I'm ready to move on to the other breast, my dick has thickened.

"Baby, can I have you again?" I say.

She lays her arms across my shoulders. "Yes…"

I lift her and press her back against the wall. She gasps when I enter her.

"Fuck," I mutter. Her fucking vaginal walls must have suction. Every thrust into her wetness pulls me closer to orgasm.

She's nibbling on my neck, and that's making me more excited. My lips find hers. Our tongues probe deep into each other's mouths. This is why I make love to her—for the giddy sensation in my heart and spinning in my head.

Angel moans, and it almost sounds like she's weeping.

"I love you," she says.

And that sends me over the cliff. Two more thrusts, and I embrace her tightly as I blast off inside her.

I WASH UP REAL QUICK, AND ANGEL ENDS HER shower on her own. Once our skin is dried and we're in bed, we hold each other tightly.

"Charlie?" Angel says in the darkness.

I embrace her tighter. "Yeah, baby?"

She's silent for a few moments. "Sleep well."

"Is that all you wanted to say?" I ask.

"Well… yeah, and thanks for going to the party with me. I know you really didn't want to. Truth be told, it wasn't all that great, especially when you weren't there."

I kiss the side of her face. "Sorry for leaving."

"It's okay."

"Oh, and I didn't tell you that I'm going to buy MOS from Jacques."

"Oh…"

We fall silent.

"Any thoughts?" I ask.

I feel her shrug against me. "I'm glad Papa is lightening his load. But…"

After few seconds I ask, "But?"

"That may mean you'll have to spend more time in LA, and so will I since we're…" Again, she falls silent.

"Together?" I ask.

"Yeah…"

We indulge in more silence. My worries slowly creep back on me. I have to tell Angel about Mita. I'll do it first thing in the morning.

"Good night, sweetie." I kiss her on the back of the head.

We snuggle closer.

"*Bonne nuit, mon amour,*" she says.

Angel turns to face me for another kiss. After the sweet act is over, I close my eyes. I thought I'd be too vexed to sleep, but I find myself very quickly drifting off.

CHAPTER SIXTEEN

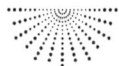

CHARLIE LORD

I take one last relaxed morning breath and open my eyes. Angel is already up and sitting against the headboard.

"Hey," I say and massage her thigh.

I would draw her beneath to feel her wet morning warmth, but it looks like she has a lot on her mind. Does Angel know about Mita and me, and has she been waiting for me to confess? Angel is patient in that way.

I rub my eyes and sit up against the headboard beside her.

"Babe…" I clear my throat. A hard knot forms in my chest.

"I'm pregnant," Angel says.

My mouth falls open. She's looking at me with such fear and confusion in her eyes.

I glance down at her stomach and then back at her face. "We have a baby in there?" I point to her stomach.

She's finally smiling, perhaps because I'm grinning.

Angel nods. "We do. That's why I wanted to get all the dancing in I could before…" She widens her eyes. "You know."

I want to hug her and show her how happy I am that we're having a kid. I never thought I'd be a father, and it was clear to both of us that having a baby wasn't even the last item on our list of priorities. As a matter of fact, we were very careful. She was on the sponge, and we were steadfast followers of the calendar method.

"Listen babe, there's something I need to tell you—now, *right now*."

A slow but unsure smile builds on her lips. "What is it?"

Where do I start? I sigh as I try to quickly figure out the answer.

"Remember a few years ago when I first started working for Jacques?"

Now she's frowning. "Yes."

"You and I were on some sort of break because I…"

Her hand moves in jerks as she runs it through her hair. "Yeah, I remember everything. Did you have sex with Monroe again?" She slaps that active hand down on her lap. "You guys had dinner the other night."

I vehemently shake my head. "No way. *No way*. That's not it. Just hear me out, will you?" I want to take her hand to assure her I will never cheat on her with another woman, but I still have a damaging confession to make.

Angel pulls her knees to her chest, hugs her legs, and nods. "Okay," she barely says.

"So I started working for Jacques, and I was feeling really good about it, but the best part of my life was missing, which was you." I look in her eyes, hoping to have scored some points, but her expression says she's expecting the worst. I take in a deep breath and let it out forcefully. I should just come out and say it. "I met Mita Capelli for the first time. She was always…" I shake my head, trying to figure out how to put it into words.

"Seducing you?" Angel says.

"Yeah…" I'm glad she said it for me.

"That's what she does. She seduces men."

"Well, she came into my room in her panties, and that's it. I had a reaction because, you know, she was naked."

I stop to read Angel's expression. It's blank.

"So…" I start again. "You know. I had never gone that long without sex, and she came over and massaged my—penis." I pause to take her temperature. One of her eyes is narrower than the other. That's her angry look.

"But I pushed her away," I add in my defense.

Angel rolls her eyes. "I imagine there's more to the story because of the state you're in."

"Okay, well the next thing I know she's sitting on my dick and riding me. It all happened so fast."

"So you fucked her?"

"Not really."

Shit, that look of scorn in her eyes makes me sick to my stomach. Actually, it's a familiar feeling.

"It only went on for seventeen seconds."

Her frown deepens. "Seventeen seconds. Were you counting?"

I go on to explain how Mita recorded the entire session and tried to use it to blackmail me.

"Her tape went on for five minutes and twenty-three seconds. She had it extended to make it look as if I was full-on fucking her. But our interaction was awkward from the start. Maggie had the tape evaluated, and… "

Angel gasps. "What? Maggie?"

"She discovered all of Mita's lies."

"What were they?" Her hand flies up. "But wait. You mean to tell me Mita actually set up a camera in your room?"

"Yes. She did."

"I heard she was poison, but I didn't know she was that poisonous. So what did Maggie find out?"

I'm not sure how I'm faring here. She's squinting, and her eyes are lit with an inner glow. "So are you mad at me?" I ask.

"No. Not yet. Keep going."

Okay… I clear my throat. "Well, um, you've heard of Sir Walter Barnaby, haven't you?"

"He's a socialite with a title."

"Right. Well, he had an affair with Ariel Hampton."

"The actress. Isn't she married to that duke?" She snaps her fingers as she thinks. "Clay Davenport?"

"Right. But Ariel Hampton had an affair with Sir Walter Barnaby, and they had a child that they wanted to keep secret, so they gave it to Mita."

Angel's mouth falls open and stays there.

"I'm not done. Mita has been using the kid to blackmail Ralph McIntyre."

Angel lets out a high-pitched yelp. "*The* Ralph McIntyre?"

"The pianist. Yeah."

I tell her how Mita convinced him that she was pregnant by him and if he didn't pay her $20,000 a month she would tell his wife.

"She wanted me to pay her twenty thousand a month too."

"Ha," Angel scoffs and scrambles to sit on her knees. "Let's go back a few deceptive steps. How did Ariel Hampton keep her pregnancy a secret? Eyes are always on her. She's an EGOT."

"A what?"

"Emmy, Grammy, Oscar, and Tony winner. She's one of the most well-known actresses in the world."

I shrug. "I don't know. Maggie didn't say. But what about us? Are you mad at me?"

She takes both of my hands and interlaces our fingers. "First of all, that was a long time ago. And yeah, we were on a strange sort of break. That was after I caught Monroe servicing you at the ski resort. I forgave you for that, didn't I?"

"I would think so."

"Remember the hospital?" She closes her eyes and shakes her head at the thought. "It was a horrible time with the loss of Joella, but I will never forget when we were in the parking garage— remember that?"

"I'll never forget it."

"I forgave you for anything you could've done to hurt me up to that day. Was Mita before that day?"

"Yes," I say poignantly.

She leans toward me, and we kiss.

"Then I forgive you," she says sweetly. Then Angel sits back and rolls her eyes. "Plus, I know Mita Capelli. She just takes what she wants. And now it all makes sense—her sneaky little smirks. She's a nasty little bitch. I can't believe she's such a brilliant cellist."

I sigh with relief and sink down from the head-board to lie on my back. "I thought you were going to leave me."

"Did you really think I was some judgmental purist who feels her man has to be faultless? I've seen Mita jump on guys at parties. She's so aggressive. Nothing you said she's done surprises me. This woman has major issues." Angel collapses on the bed as if that last tirade sapped her of energy.

"Well, she told your cousin, Anton. He talked to

me about it last night. Just like Maggie, he urged me to tell you the truth, but he added an 'or else' clause."

"Or else he'd tell me himself?"

"Yeah."

Angel takes my hand, and we massage each other's palms.

"That explains why he's been so weird about you. I can't believe she went and told him. I'm sure she wanted him to be PR."

"PR?"

"The disseminator of her news."

"Oh…"

"Yeah. But Anton doesn't spread rumors. He's one of a kind, like you."

I study every pore and line of Angel's smooth face. As usual, her eyes are bright and optimistic. I can hardly fucking believe that we're having a child together. I couldn't ask the Lord God Almighty for a better partner to walk through this world with.

Angel pets the side of my face. "Hey, baby, are you okay?"

"I've never been more okay than I am now." I scoot to the edge of the bed. "I want to do something. Can I take you somewhere?"

"Where?"

"It's a surprise."

She rubs her hands together. "You know I'm always up for one of your surprises."

"Then I'll make some calls, and then we're out of here."

Her face still beaming, Angel springs onto her knees. Being a dancer makes her so agile and limber. "Out of where? Bordeaux?"

I tilt my head and narrow an eye suspiciously. "Damn, you're good, but I told you it's a surprise."

Her shoulders slump. "Okay, you caught me. But I'm excited," she says, grinning to the max.

"First…" I strike like a snake and draw her up under me. "My appetite, and I'm not talking food."

"Ah…" she says, intrigued, and shrugs her eyebrows. "Then eat me."

I use my knee to part her legs. It doesn't take long for my wood to grow.

"Shit," I whimper as I thrust myself inside her morning delight. "Fuck." One thrust, and it won't be long before I burst. Two and a half years into this relationship, and I'm still slain by her pussy.

CHAPTER SEVENTEEN

MAGGIE ADAMS

*F*our days straight on this mission, and I'm so exhausted that I'm struggling to keep my eyes open. Two suites at the Royal Grande Seine hotel were booked—one to hold the adults in this matter, and the other for the child. My hope is that we can come to some initial understanding of what's best for the child today.

"So what do you think?" I ask.

Dr. Luc Calvet and I are standing in the foyer, observing Abel Rinaldi. He was given the same last name as Mita's great grandfather—go figure. Before I arrived, Dr. Calvet spent time with Abel and Laura McIntyre. He noticed some distance between them as well as something else that alarmed him. He was sure that the child displayed anxiety around

Laura, who had been very distant from Abel ever since discovering he was not her brother's child. And so three hours before my flight landed, Dr. Calvet contacted me to ask who'd spent the most time with the child. I assumed it was the nanny.

"Then she must come," he said.

So I worked with agents on the ground to bring Aida, the nanny, to the hotel. At first, Aida was afraid because she knew Mita's secret and felt that she was a party to her employer's lies. But Aida's agents put her in touch with me, and I assured her that I was working to make a better life for the child and no harm would come to her.

"Are you American?" she asked.

"Yes, but don't let that scare you," I said with a chuckle.

That broke the ice. She chuckled too, and a car was sent to Bondy, where she lives, to pick her up. Now Aida's in the living room with Abel, helping him play with building blocks.

"The child is more responsive with Aida. He has no anxiety when he is with her, and that is very good. But he shows signs of lack of stimulation."

I cross my arms and observe Abel more. He's cute as a button—chubby cheeks, big blue eyes, and red lips. However, although he's playing with the blocks, it doesn't look like he's having any fun. He's just doing his duty, following orders, surviving. He doesn't seem to notice Aida sitting there, and she's as distant as a long road to nowhere. The sight causes my heart to break.

"My guess is Aida has been his primary caregiver, but she has six children of her own and is unable to care for him properly."

"Fuck," I say under my breath. Dr. Calvet looks at me as if he's evaluating my mood. I tap him on the shoulder to let him know that I'm fine. "It's just that I read through the file I was sent on Aida, and she wasn't paid much to take care of him. I can imagine how she treated him."

Dr. Calvet shakes his head adamantly. "No, no, no… from my quick evaluation, I detect the nanny was not cruel to the child, yet not so affectionate either. She was more…" He rolls his hand as if he's searching to come up with an expression I might understand. "She was more dutiful."

"I see." I sigh. "Well, it's time to get Abel back to his biological parents."

Dr. Calvet nods in agreement.

"By the way, thank you for taking this case on such short notice."

"You are welcome," he says.

"I'll be back," I say with a nod.

He purses his lips and nods too.

I walk over to the room next door where, Laura McIntyre, Sir Walter Barnaby, and Ariel Hampton are being detained. Peter, a burly man in a black suit who's our muscle, opens the door when he sees me.

"Bonjour," I say.

As soon as I'm inside, I hear a woman asking why she can't leave. "I don't want the child."

"Soon, madam," an official-sounding voice says.

When I walk into the living room, Sir Walter Barnaby and Ariel Hampton shoot to their feet. They look exhausted by the proceedings.

"Are you the one who had them bring me here?" Laura McIntyre says.

Her face is red, eyes beady, and mouth tight. In general, she looks as if she frowns more than smiles. I think back to the phone logs. Laura didn't want to smuggle Abel out of the country because she loved him—she wanted to win against Mita. Unfortunately, she had no clue Mita didn't care an ounce for the child.

I straighten my posture and walk with authority. "Sit down," I say.

"No. Why am I here with them? Isn't she an

actress? And he's… I don't know what he does. He's just known for nothing. Not only do I want out of here, but I will sue for every dime Ralph has paid that bitch."

"Sit the fuck down," I command, looking her strongly in the eye.

Her lips part, and she gasps, offended. She's an entitled bitch.

"You were attempting to kidnap a child and steal him out of the country when you were detained," I say. "So walk out that door, and you will be taken into custody. And that's a promise."

"We've remained silent like you asked," Sir Walter says.

I gather he's trying to take my sting out of the air. But I don't acknowledge him. I keep my hardened expression on Laura until she smoothes her herringbone trousers and takes a seat.

"Great." I smile, satisfied. "You'll be able to leave as soon as we reach an understanding."

Laura shakes her head and sighs. She's a defiant one.

"Your brother paid Miss Capelli for a reason. He thought he had a secret to keep. He, in fact, did carry on an affair with her for six sex-filled months. I have evidence that's stronger than receipts and selfies—although I have those too." I wink at her.

She scratches her scalp impatiently. "Then what do you have?"

"Miss Capelli did present true proof to Mr. McIntyre that he had impregnated her." I dig through my leather saddlebag and take out a copy of Mita's medical record. I hand it to Laura, who's more cooperative now that we've gotten the show on the road.

Laura scans the form, frowning.

"Pay attention to the red xs," I say. "First, you'll see that a paternity test was done on a fetus. The second x confirms Ralph McIntyre has a ninety-nine-point-nine-percent chance of being the father. However…" I hand Laura a second form. Sir Walter and Ariel watch my every move. I can tell they're becoming more confident in my ability to handle their secret as I move forward in this process. "This is an easier document to figure out.

"Aborted?"

"Yes." I point to Ariel and Sir Walter. "Meet Abel's real parents."

Laura stares at them incredulously.

I nod at Sir Walter, giving him permission to say

what we rehearsed while I was flying over the Atlantic.

"We are prepared to pay Mr. McIntyre…"

"What kind of people would leave their child with that conniving, manipulative, low-rate whore?" Laura stares at Ariel expectantly.

Ariel turns away to gaze out the window. There's something about her demeanor that I find troubling. She has agreed to come clean with her husband and share custody with Sir Walter, who has also agreed to break the news to his wife. But I sense some apprehension on her part.

"Laura," I say.

She looks at me.

"Sir Walter has agreed to reimburse Mr. McIntyre whatever was paid to Mita, plus interest."

Laura still has that distant look in her eyes, as if she's putting the pieces together regarding Abel's biological parents. I take my cell phone out of my bag and hit two, two, three to speed dial Ralph McIntyre and put it on speakerphone.

"Yes, hello," he says as though he's been expecting my call.

"Hello, Mr. McIntyre. It's me, Maggie Adams. We're here with your sister, Laura."

"Laura, don't give them any trouble," he says in

the accent of an American who's been in England for a very long time. "I've agreed to their terms, and I don't want to hear any more of it, understand?"

Laura sighs bitterly and glares across the room at Ariel and Sir Walter. "I understand very well."

"Good. You understand that any of this getting to the press will hurt me, and you too?"

She slaps a hand on her chest. "Me?"

"You were attempting to kidnap a child, and we have proof," I say.

"I don't care. I won't say a word. I want this over and done with. I want to leave. May I?"

I rip my gaze away from her nasty stare. "Thank you, Mr. McIntyre. I'm very happy we could come to an agreement, and your name will be removed from any records claiming you as father of the child."

He pauses for a few beats, then his voice cracks when he says, "Thank you."

I end the call and turn to Laura. "You may leave."

She shoots to her feet, hangs her purse over her shoulder, and saunters away without taking a second glance at any of us.

"By the way, a car will take you to wherever

you'd like to go." My tone indicates that it's not personal but business.

Laura stops but doesn't turn around. "Thank you," she says and walks out the door.

Now I'm alone with my clients.

Ariel stands. "I can't."

"He's your child," I say, disgusted by her selfishness.

"I gave him up. A nice family will adopt him."

Sir Walter crosses his legs. "That is not going to happen. I've been living with this for too long. He's my child."

"Ha!" Ariel says, mocking him. "Helene is a mean bitch. She will treat our son like a slave. She can't have him—I won't let her." She sits back down to look him pleadingly in the eyes. "Abel needs a family, Walter. Why did you give him to Mita Capelli in the first place?" She looks at me with an expression that begs for understanding. "I didn't know who Walter gave him to. He told me our son was with a good family."

"I didn't know either," Sir Walter barks.

"Okay," I say. "Mita lied to everyone, but where will this child go if not with you?"

Ariel sighs forcefully as she stands. "This will stay in this room, will it?"

Goodness. I want to lay into her for being a self-ish, loveless woman. That poor kid.

"It will," I mutter past clenched teeth.

"Walter, Helene will make that child's life miserable, and you will let her. You've hired Maggie to fix this problem. Now fix it. But we're not the parents."

I look at Sir Walter Barnaby. He's staring into my eyes, but the moment he looks down at his lap, I know exactly what he's going to do. I shake my head and close my eyes. I'm not even sure I want to try to talk sense into them. Ages two to ten are the formative years. All these two people can put into that innocent child who's just trying to survive are anger, confusion, and horrible feelings of being unloved. So I'm unable to speak without cursing and yelling at these selfish parents. I nod at them, turn my back, and walk out of the room.

TWO HOURS LATER

"Thank you, baby," I say to Vince, but I can't stop crying my eyes out.

Before I left the hotel, I went into the next room to pay the nanny and thank her for her time.

"What will happen to him?" she asked.

"He'll be adopted," I said.

I was silent for a long moment as I watched Abel, who was still playing with the blocks. I thought, *Aren't two-year-olds supposed to be running around the room, touching everything and looking for snacks?* Next, I considered making the greatest sacrifice of my life. Tears flowed freely from my eyes. Not even a small part of me could walk away from this sad little boy who didn't even know how to be a two-year-old.

When I turned to face Aida again, she nodded at me. I could tell she knew what I had decided.

"Good luck," she said. "He is a good boy, a very good boy."

We hugged, she left, and I looked at Dr. Calvet, who'd been observing me silently.

"You are in New York—Manhattan, right?"

"Yes."

"I will see you there to begin a session in…" He took out his phone and scrolled the screen. "How is next Monday for you?"

"Are you coming to New York?"

"I'd like to. Like you, I would like to help Abel. And what you've chosen to do can only be done by a heart that is pure love."

I swallowed hard, scared out of my mind. I had no idea how to be a mother, but one thing I knew for sure—Vince and I would never hurt the child.

So I called Vince and started from the beginning. He knew exactly what I was leading to before I could make it to the end. He asked if I was ready and went down the list, step by step, of how my life would change.

"I guess I'll take local clients only," I said.

He fell silent and then said, "Well, then, I can't wait to officially meet our new son."

We're working on the official adoption, but I was granted special permission to take the child with me. Jack has always had friends in high places, and I've benefitted greatly from those heights, starting with my job at A&Rt Media, where Vince and I reconnected and fell in love. And if it weren't for Mita blackmailing Charlie, and Jack's whole covert network that helped me bring down her house of cards, I never would've had the opportunity to rescue this poor baby before life made him another angry and messed-up human being on the planet.

"We'll be okay—don't worry," Vince says.

I sigh and look down at Abel, who's in a

comfortable high chair beside me. His face is covered in white cheese sauce. "I know."

"What is he doing now?"

I chuckle. "Eating fresh basil and creamy white cheddar fettuccine."

He laughs. "Fancy meal for a two-year-old."

"He'll be doing a lot of fancy things for a little while. That's until we figure out how to go at the right speed."

For the first time since we've been together, Abel looks up at me with a smile.

"You know what?" I say to Vince.

"What?"

"I think we have an old soul on our hands."

Abel really giggles now.

"I hear him," Vince says.

And we all share our first laugh together.

CHAPTER EIGHTEEN

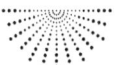

CHARLIE LORD

e're on the tail end of a thirteen-hour flight. Angel and I slept most of the flight. Releasing that vexing secret took all the tension out of me. After four days of nonstop stress, my body could finally relax. Then the ringing of the cabin phone awakened us. I panicked slightly when I saw it was Jack, thinking he was calling to tell us that Daisy was in the hospital having the baby. I would've had to divert our plans for another time, but that wasn't the case. Instead, he delivered news so shocking that I shook my head several times, thinking I would wake myself out of this dream.

"What?" I say.

"Maggie's adopting a child, a little boy. He's two and a half years old," Jack says.

I'm waiting for him to finish the joke. But Jack rarely ever jokes around and definitely not about something like that.

"What does Maggie know about raising a kid?" Then it suddenly dawns on me. "What the hell do I know about raising a kid? By the way…" Every time I think about it, I grin. "Angel's pregnant."

"Yeah?" Jack says. But there's no surprise or excitement in his voice.

"You knew, didn't you?"

He's silent for a second. "Angel told Daisy four weeks ago. I was ordered not to say anything."

I tilt my head and narrow an eye playfully at Angel, who slaps a hand over her mouth and shrugs.

"Believe me, when I first heard, I was afraid for the kid." He laughs, and so do I. "But then I shook it off. You and Angel are going to be fine parents, and now our kid will have a cousin to play with."

"Like Maggie," I say, grinning.

"Yeah…"

I wonder if Jack is thinking what I'm thinking: we're going to be way better fathers than our father.

"So where are you going?" Jack asks.

I shift in my seat. "Can't tell you, brother, but how about we meet in Manhattan this weekend and welcome the new addition to the family, Lord style?"

"Daisy could go into labor any day now, but we were thinking about making that trip regardless. We're going to move to the Vineyard for a while."

"Oh yeah? Why?"

"We're opening a bakery," Jack says.

"On Circuit Street?"

"Yeah."

Rex, the pilot, tells us to prepare for landing. These days, Jack and I are used to having long conversations, but now we have to cut it short. I tell him I'll see him on Saturday at Vince's penthouse. I wonder if they're going to remain in Vince's extravagant apartment in the sky now that they've taken on a two-and-a-half-year-old kid. There are a thousand ways a rambunctious toddler could kill himself in that place.

Angel and I raise our eyebrows at each other, still absorbing the news.

"I never pictured myself with children, and I surely never pictured Maggie with any," Angel says. "She's an extreme worker bee."

"I guess fate knows when it's time to slow a person down," I say from experience.

"You're so right." Angel claps twice. "Okay, Charles, spill the beans. Where are you taking me?"

I'm saved by Chloe, who walks out of the back compartment to clear our trash and make sure our seatbelts are fastened.

"You'll know very soon," I say.

Angel squeezes my hand. "All right, I'll have patience. But I know we're definitely back in the US. I can feel it in the air."

"Prepare for landing," the pilot says.

Angel and I look at each other and then hold hands. I swear that at least a hundred times a day, her beauty stuns me.

THE AIRCRAFT LANDS, AND SOON CHLOE AND SAM let down the ramp. Bright light whisks into the cabin.

"Wait," Angel says, walking toward it after I take her weekender bag from her. "I recognize this light. We're in the desert." She makes it to the door. "Holy hell, Charlie…" She whips her stunned gaze to me. "Las Vegas?"

I walk to her and embrace her, holding her tightly. "Angel, will you marry me today?"

Her forehead wrinkles and then smoothes as her mouth stretches into the most beautiful smile on the planet. "How do you always manage to read my mind?"

I kiss her. "Then we're going to do it?"

Angel dances in place. "Let's do it!" She slaps a hand over her chest. "But wait. We're not dressed for a wedding."

She's wearing a yellow spaghetti-strapped maxi dress, one of my favorite of her outfits. I'm in my black pants and baby-blue lightweight polo shirt.

"We look fine," I say.

Angel examines both of our outfits. "I guess so, and who cares, right?"

Claps erupt. We turn to see Chloe, Sam, Captain Dozier, and his copilot, Captain Bland, applauding.

We wave to our audience and skip down the ramp to the white Mercedes Benz limousine that's waiting for us. After our luggage is loaded into the trunk, we race northward to the chapel, which is at the end of Las Vegas Boulevard. Angel and I make out in the back seat during the ride.

When we make it to the chapel, two readymade

bridesmaids sweep Angel to the dressing room, and I quickly finish up the licensing paperwork that I had prepared earlier. Soon, I'm in front of Elvis. The organist is playing a sloppy rendition of the wedding march—I think on purpose—and Angel appears at the top of the aisle wearing a veil and too much makeup and carrying a bouquet of flowers. She's laughing at herself, and I chuckle too, even though I'm so happy I could fucking cry. This woman is about to become mine, all mine. I won't be able to believe it until we say those final words, "I do."

Finally, Angel approaches me. The organist plays a snappy rendition of "The Little White Chapel," and Elvis is shaking his leg and jerking his chest while singing along. Halfway down the aisle, Angel shimmies toward me, and I shimmy toward her. We meet and dance together until I dip her when Elvis sings his final note.

Now that that's over, we run to our spots, and Elvis begins the ceremony.

"Dearly beloved," he starts, and we laugh. "We are gathered here today in this holy, angelic metropolis of Sin City…" Elvis clears his throat. "I meant to say *Las Vegas*, to join Charles Edward Lord

II and Angelina Marie Beauchamp in holy matrimony."

We beam, gazing into each other's eyes.

"Now, vows are sacred in the eyes of God," Elvis says. "He knows your heart, and he told me that your hearts are full of love for each other."

"Amen, amen, amen…" shouts a woman in a grey wig and flowery dress who's sitting in the pews, clutching a bible to her chest.

Angel giggles. I can tell she's having a ball.

"Why, yes. Amen," Elvis says in his customary accent, which is a riot to listen to. This guy is good —very good. "All right, now, let's just get to it. Charles Edward Lord II, do you take this fine specimen of a woman to be your lawfully wedded wife, to have and to hold from this day forward, for better or for worse, richer or poorer, through sickness and in health until death do you part?"

Tears rush to my eyes when he says that. This is all in fun, but those words are mimicking my heart exactly. "With all my heart, I do," I say, choked up.

Tears roll from my eyes, and Angel brushes them away.

"And you, Angelina Marie Beauchamp—beautiful name by the way. Are you sure you don't want to run away with old Elvis here instead?" He's nudging himself in the chest with his thumb while giving her a cartoonish smile.

Angel giggles. "Not in a million years," she declares as she squeezes my hands tighter.

Elvis winks. "Had to try."

I wink at him. "I would too, if I were in your shoes."

He laughs heartily. "Well, let's get to it, shall we?"

"Let's," Angel says, beaming at me.

"Angelina Marie Beauchamp. Do you take Charles Edward Lord II as your lawfully wedded husband, to have and to hold from this day forward, for better or for worse, richer or poorer, through sickness and in health until death do you part?"

"I do," Angel cries jubilantly.

"Then Charles Edward Lord II and Angelina Marie Beauchamp, you have officially spoken your vows in the sight of God and can now file your joint tax returns for the state. So now go on, son, and kiss your beautiful bride!"

We laugh at Elvis's spectacular ending to a well-deliberated wedding, and then I plant the biggest kiss I've ever given on Angel.

We don't end our classic Vegas wedding day there. We're driven to the Golden Nugget's buffet and eat as much fatty and greasy prime rib and dried-out fish as we can before heading up to our luxury spa tower suite.

First, we strip out of our sweaty clothes and take a bubble bath, which has already been prepared for us. I drink champagne, and Angel drinks melon water with crushed mint and lime.

"So, Mrs. Lord, how does it feel to be a married woman?"

Angel's expression turns sultry. She sets her glass down and moves in my direction until our noses touch. "It feels amazing." Her lips merge with mine, and we kiss until she straddles my lap to sit on my rigid dick.

"Mr. Lord…" She closes her eyes and moans as she bites her lower lip. "How does it feel to be inside your new wife?"

"Like Heaven, baby." She's not shifting her hips, and it's frustrating the hell out of me. But then her perfect tits are above my nose, so I pull one of them into my watery mouth. She moans, which tells me she's enjoying my stimulation. I've learned not to be so greedy about eating her tits.

"Let's take this to the bedroom," she whispers in my ear.

I nod wildly. "Yeah."

Sparks shoot through my dick as she stands and takes me out of her. Damn, I love being inside her. Once we're out of the tub, I pick her up and put my wood back where it was before we left the water.

"Shit," I mutter. She feels so fucking good.

I carry my bride to one of the guest rooms in the suite, lay her on the bed, and make love to her. This is the beginning of our nonstop sex session. Pretty soon, our baby will grow larger, so for now, I do Angel in every way possible. She's on her knees. I'm entering her from the side. Then sixty-nine. We make up positions as we go. She blows me and doesn't stop until I come, *hard*. Then I eat her pussy until she withers from climaxing so much.

Before nightfall, we make it back to the main bedroom, snuggle up close, and fall asleep. Hours later, my cell phone chimes. I have a text message. Angel stirs. I squint at the clock. It's 7:43 a.m.

"Morning, sweetie," I say.

She rubs my thigh, her eyes still closed. "Morning."

I reach over to get my phone off the nightstand, careful not to overstretch—I want Angel's hand to stay where it is. After checking this message, my dick is going back to its favorite place.

"It's a message from Jack," I say.

"Oh…" Angel opens her eyes. "What does it say?"

"Daisy's in labor. And he's given us the address to the hospital in San Francisco."

Angel is fully alert as she sits straight up. "Then we have to go."

I tug her toward me and guide her up under me. "We will, but first…" I raise my brow suggestively, basically asking if she could take this moment to have sex before flying out of Vegas.

"Okay, but let's make it quick."

I thrust myself into her morning wetness and warmth. "That won't be a problem," I say with a sigh as sensations stir in my dick on first thrust.

Angel whimpers with delight, and her delicious pussy finishes me off in time for us to get out of here and make a flight to San Francisco.

TWO WEEKS LATER

Daisy and Jack had a boy and named him Charles Edward Lord III. Maggie and Vince brought Abel to Montecito, where Daisy is recovering, and Angel and I are here too. We're all sitting around the pool in the backyard while Jack's cook grills steaks.

Angel has just relieved Maggie of the duty of teaching Abel how to swim. Now he's splashing and laughing as he swims from Vince to Angel.

I've never seen Maggie's face so full and bright. "He's good, isn't he?"

Daisy cradles Ed in her arms—that's what we call the new baby. "Who, Vince or Abel?"

"Both," Maggie says. "Vince is an excellent teacher. We started swim lessons with Abel as a form of therapy, and let me tell you, he's come leaps and bounds from the scared little boy he was a few weeks ago."

"It's love," Daisy says, looking down at Ed. "It can move mountains if we let it."

Maggie goes on about therapy with Dr. Luc Calvet.

"Abel is just so happy. He calls me 'Mom' and Vince 'Dad.' I thought it would be difficult to adjust, but it's not. Then there are all of these things we're afraid of—like Vince not wanting to be a hard-ass like his dad was to him or me not wanting to be absent like my mom was. Dr. Calvet says it's about balance and learning to let Abel lead and giving him what he needs and wants while still maintaining boundaries. There's a lot to learn, just a lot."

Jack and I glance at each other. Our dad was the king of hard-asses.

"Looks like you're learning it," Jack says.

Maggie cracks a tiny smile. "We certainly are."

Jack holds out his hands toward Daisy. "Can I have him?"

"Of course, babe." Ed whines a little during the exchange. "Go to Daddy."

As soon as my nephew's in Jack's arms, he settles against his father's chest as though it's a known comfortable spot for him.

Maggie tears her smile away from father and son and directs it at me. "So, Chuck, I heard you're moving back to LA."

The thought of my next big step makes me grin. "Yeah… Angel's going to work on a few story-editing projects. I'm giving her an office at the studio."

"Oh," Maggie says, sounding intrigued. "You're working together?"

"I guess you can say that."

"Hey, just want to let you know that I'm pretty proud of you, Charlie," Jack says.

For some reason, the sincerity in his expression chokes me up. Jack has always been more like a father to me than a brother. I'll probably seek his approval for the rest of my life, and it won't be so hard won.

"Thank you, Jack. That means a lot to me," I manage to say without my voice cracking.

He nods and then kisses Ed gently on top of the head.

"Did you ever think we'd be here together like this?" Maggie says.

"You mean with two kids between us and one on the way?" I say. "Nope."

We laugh.

"Yet here we are," Jack says.

"Yep," Maggie and I say at the same time.

"Yep," Jack repeats.

"Go, go, go!" Angel and Vince chant cheerfully.

Vince holds Abel, who looks as if he thinks he's swimming like a pro on his own. We laugh and cheer with them. It's a great moment in time, and all I can hope is that we have more like it.

READ HOW IT ALL TURNS OUT IN THE FINAL BOOK OF THE LOVE IN THE USA SERIES FEATURING THE LORDS. GET IT NOW!

Adore Her, More of Her (Daisy & Belmont, #2)

Book 10